De

Jo ripped ope _____ _____ ___ ___ gosh, check this out," s_e demanded, heart rate accelerating faster than a zillion horsepower engine. "Natascia, here's to fast cars and faster friendships. Antonio. Ohhh, couldn't you just *die?*"

"Pretty profound," Theresa said, focusing her gaze on the Godiva chocolates. "Pass 'em over."

"So how well do you know this guy?" Caylin asked. "Don't forget, Jonathon thinks a *translator* planted the bugs. And that more than likely means you, Jo. Maybe Antonio is one of Jonathon's cronies."

"Antonio has nothing to do with Jonathon," Jo said, rolling her eyes. "I know him well enough, I assure you. Now which one should I have first? The pink one or the heart-shaped chocolate one?"

"Come on, you guys!" Caylin cried. "Jo's life could be in danger here. *All* our lives could be in danger now that this Antonio guy knows where we *are!* Doesn't that matter to you?"

"Not where chocolate's concerned," Theresa said.

Don't miss any books in this thrilling new series:

Available from ARCHWAY Paperbacks

SPY GiRLS

License to Thrill

by
Elizabeth Cage

AN ARCHWAY PAPERBACK
Published by POCKET BOOKS

New York   London   Toronto   Sydney   Tokyo   Singapore

AN ARCHWAY PAPERBACK *Original*

An Archway Paperback published by
POCKET BOOKS, a division of Simon & Schuster Inc.
1230 Avenue of the Americas, New York, NY 10020

Produced by 17th Street Productions, a division of
Daniel Weiss Associates, Inc., New York

ISBN: 0-671-002286-5

First Archway Paperback printing October 1998

10 9 8 7 6 5 4 3 2 1

AN ARCHWAY PAPERBACK and colophon are
registered trademarks of Simon & Schuster Inc.

Printed in the U.S.A.

IL 7+

To Jay Brown, my superfly Spy Guy

This is the *life*." Caylin Pike sighed as she leaned her blond head back against the plush Royal Airways seat. "There's nothing like sitting in first class to make a trip to England extra comfy."

"You're telling me," Jo Carreras exclaimed. "I mean, the service is out of control. I think I've already drunk my weight in diet Coke, and we've only been in the air for an hour." Her ebony eyes gleamed mischievously as she hit the reading light button. Its golden glow shone down on her face, highlighting her cheekbones and rich, flawless complexion.

"I never knew how lame flying coach was until now," Theresa Hearth added with a luxurious yawn as she extended her long, tan legs in front of her. "What's the ETA?"

"Um, I *believe* we have about five hours to go," Caylin replied with a roll of her baby blues. She'd made who-knew-how-many cross-Atlantic journeys in her seventeen years on the planet, and the reminder that she'd be rooted in her seat for that long made first class suddenly feel far from comfy. She squirmed restlessly, wondering how to inject some excitement into the long ride ahead. Other than jumping out the emergency door and surfing 747 style to the land of fish-and-chips, she couldn't imagine how.

Jo let out a long sigh from the center seat. "If only there were some U.K.-variety hotties on this plane—then we could *really* make time fly. Where's Gavin Rossdale when you need him?"

Caylin laughed. "Jo, don't your babedar batteries *ever* wear out?"

"Nope!" Theresa broke in. "They keep going . . . and going . . . and going. . . ." She craned her makeup-free face up over the seat back in front of her and scanned the first-class compartment. "Whoa, Jo, check out that cutie in two-B. I bet he's Gavin's long lost twin."

Caylin chuckled as she eyed the object of Theresa's joking affections—a gray-haired guy a couple of rows ahead.

"Cut it out," Jo complained. "You shouldn't get my hopes up like that. I *don't* go for the geriatric set, thankyouverymuch."

"Oh, so you *are* selective," Caylin drawled. "I was beginning to wonder. . . ." She trailed off as she realized that the gentleman in question had turned to stare at her, causing her face to make like a fire engine. "Okay, you guys, change of subject," she whispered hastily.

"Got one," Jo began. "What do you think our first mission is going to be?"

I wish I knew, Caylin thought, her heart

pounding in anticipation of the adventure that lay ahead for her and her two new gal pals. Just four months ago Caylin, fresh out of high school in Maine, had been recruited by The Tower, a super-secret organization that was rumored to be a joint venture between the CIA and the FBI.

Hardly what I expected, Caylin noted silently as she recalled arriving in Washington, D.C., for what she had been led to believe was a post-high-school, see-the-world-while-you-help-it program like the Peace Corps. She had been all set to use her extensive mountaineering skills to teach underprivileged Tibetans how to become more self-sufficient or maybe employ her clout as a champion snowboarder to bring excitement to the sunlight-deprived lives of teenagers in Iceland.

Instead she was hit by an unexpected bombshell. Top secret government operatives had been watching Caylin since the seventh grade with the idea that she would someday make a perfect international spy for the U.S. government—and right there by her side in D.C. had been Jo and Theresa, two complete strangers who had undergone the same scrutiny.

Once they had set foot through The Tower's doors, she, Jo, and Theresa had to put their "normal" teenage lives behind them forever. Now, with sixteen weeks of Bond-style training under their collective belts, the trio were on their first real mission. In the short time they'd known one another the newly christened Spy Girls had become best buds—and, Caylin hoped, an awesome team.

We definitely work well together, Caylin thought. Her ability to put on a good act for authority figures—honed over years spent sneaking out past curfew for late night street skating—blended perfectly with Theresa's high-tech problem-solving prowess and Jo's expert knowledge of foreign languages. But Caylin couldn't help wondering if friendship and teamwork would be enough to sustain them through a mission they hadn't been told one iota about.

Let the fish-and-chips fall where they may, baby, she resolved, a smile of barely suppressed excitement playing on her lips. I'm ready to go wherever the wind carries me—and I can't wait to get there!

"I bet it's some sort of unsolved murder," Theresa guessed. "Maybe in a school. That way we can pretend to be students and go undercover. Get the inside scoop."

"Mmmm, that would work for me," Jo breathed, her tone growing dreamy. "I can see it now— London prep schools, yummy boys in uniforms, those awesome accents. . . ."

"But why would the U.S. government get involved in something like that?" Caylin asked. "Think about it—we're going to the U.K. I heard the British government is cracking down on their out-of-control tabloids, so perhaps the U.S. is trying to help out. Maybe we're going to pose as paparazzi to find out what kind of practices go on behind closed doors."

"That would be cool," Theresa said. "Plus it doesn't sound *too* dangerous."

"Hey, I'm looking for danger," Caylin exclaimed. "Those paparazzi can get kinda nasty."

"*Completely* nasty," Jo agreed. "They can put on a pretty good chase—and I'm all into that."

Theresa shook her head. "Not me. You guys may be thrill seekers, but I'm a thrill *freaker*." Her stomach lurched as she imagined how she would function in a truly tense situation—one where she wouldn't have time to analyze, only act. Sure, she'd had plenty of experience during her Tower training, but now for the first time she'd be expected to perform in a totally uncontrolled environment.

Trial by fire, she thought, glowering. Not my style at all. There was no question in Theresa's mind that her partners would be able to get the job—*any* job—done and have a fantabulous time along the way. But Theresa, a computer fiend her entire life back in Arizona, was more used to working on the sidelines than being in the eye of the storm, and she dealt far better with inanimate objects than with real people—not to mention people who could put her head on a silver platter.

"Well, we'll just have to loosen you up, girl," Jo enthused.

"Yeah," Caylin agreed. "A few days in London with us and you'll be looking at danger in a *totally* new light."

"Hey, speaking of looking," Jo began, "that guy is still staring at us."

"What guy?" Theresa and Caylin asked in stereo.

"My new *boyfriend,* remember?"

Theresa inched up slightly in her window seat. Sure enough, the gray-haired guy she'd joked about earlier had his eyes on her like white on rice. She shivered, her mind racing with possible theories as to why this total stranger would find three teenage chicks so fascinating.

Sinking down slowly, Theresa whispered, "Do you think he's . . . on to us? Like, he knows who we are or something?"

"Let's not freak quite yet," Caylin replied, her tone suddenly all business. "We'll just monitor his movements and figure out what to do from there."

"Sounds like a plan, Stan." Jo ran a manicured hand through her glossy black locks and exhaled deeply. "Look—he's reaching for the Airfone."

"Maybe we should listen in on his phone call," Caylin suggested.

"Can you rig up our Airfone to tap into his?" Jo asked Theresa.

She shook her head sadly. "Dang, no. My gear's stashed down below."

Caylin leaned into the aisle, her eyebrows furrowing in concentration. "Shhh—he's muttering something," she whispered. "And it ain't English."

Jo leaned an ear between the seats. "It's French," she diagnosed. "I'll translate. No prob."

As the swoosh of the man's credit card through the Airfone's pay slot echoed ominously in Theresa's ears, Jo casually set her drink on Theresa's tray, motioned for Caylin to get up, and scooted past her into the aisle. Theresa's heart thump thump thumped out of control as Jo snuck up the red-carpeted aisle, slid into the seat behind Mr. Suspicious, and pretended to search for a magazine in its deep velvet pocket.

Caylin glanced at Theresa and shrugged. "That guy's speaking way too fast," she whispered. "I can't make out a word. Then again, I was never at the top of my class *français*-wise."

Theresa nodded. "The only French I've ever mastered involves fries, so I'm totally lost." She watched nervously as Jo glued her twice-pierced ear to the back of the guy's seat. Suddenly Jo's sparkling eyes lit up, and a smile played on her pouty lips.

"What could she possibly be smiling at?" Caylin murmured. "This isn't a game, for Pete's sake!"

Theresa shook her head, dumbfounded. "Beats me."

The man quickly hung up the phone, and Theresa's blood ran cold with worry. But Jo simply sauntered back to her seat. Forced casualness, Theresa noted unhappily. We're sunk!

"So what'd he say?" Caylin demanded, her blue eyes glittering with impatience.

Theresa gnawed on her thumbnail. "He's on to us, right?"

"Well, he *did* mention us several times," Jo began as she reclaimed her drink from Theresa's tray and took a sip.

"Oh no," Theresa lamented, her mind ticking off countless scenarios, none of them good.

"I *knew* it!" Caylin whispered, her fists clenched tightly. "Who does he work for?"

"Weeelllllll," Jo drawled, "he said he couldn't help looking at us because . . ."

"What is it already, Jo?" Caylin snarled. "Spit it out!"

"I don't think you can handle it," Jo said gravely.

"Please, just get it over with," Theresa begged.

Jo took a deep breath. "Okay. I don't know how you're going to take this, but . . . apparently we remind that guy of his daughters, and we've made him feel horribly homesick."

"What?" Caylin cried, sending Jo into a fit of self-satisfied giggles.

Theresa leaned back in her seat and exhaled slowly. "Please, don't *ever* do that again, Jo. You almost gave me a heart attack."

Caylin punched Jo on the arm. "*Not* cool, Jo," she complained. "I was about ready to go over and take care of the guy myself."

"Okay, I'm sorry for bugging you guys out," Jo apologized. "Maybe it wasn't cool, but it was a much needed reality check. We can't let paranoia get the best of us, and we shouldn't freak out without good reason."

"A little paranoia can be helpful sometimes," Theresa murmured as she gazed out the window. There wasn't much to look at—they had flown into the middle of the night, and she couldn't see anything but lacy gray clouds against the black sky. How many more bizarro situations am I going to end up in? she wondered, biting her lip. And how many of them *aren't* going to be false alarms?

"Here you go," the flight attendant said as she woke Jo from a long nap and handed her a videotape. "Special delivery."

"What is it?" Jo asked with a yawn. She couldn't recall ordering a video—not even in her sleep. But the woman had already disappeared down the aisle.

As Jo began examining the tape Caylin stirred awake and squinted into the bright sunlight streaming through the window. Meanwhile Theresa napped on, lightly snoring.

Jo nudged Theresa with her elbow. "Wakey wake," she sang. "Looks like we have some viewing material here."

Caylin grabbed the tape out of Jo's hands and studied the label. "*Three American Werewolves in London,*" she read with a laugh. "Obviously from The Tower."

Theresa snorted. "I'm offended!"

"Well, we *can* transform ourselves in the blink

of an eye," Caylin offered. "You know, with disguises."

"And I love wearing fur as long as it's fake," Jo added. She took the vid back from Caylin and popped it into the combination TV-VCR embedded in the seat back before her.

"Hopefully we'll finally find out what we're supposed to be *doing*," Caylin said as she rushed to hit the play button. "Earphones, everyone."

A shot of a black limousine filled the screen and the rich voice of Uncle Sam, their boss, filled the silence. "Good morning, Spy Girls," he intoned. "You're almost there."

Jo impulsively hit pause. "Doesn't he sound too gorgeous?" she swooned. Ever since Jo had first heard Uncle Sam's voice, she'd been dying to meet him. But neither she nor her two partners had ever been allowed to see Uncle Sam's face—it seemed to be the most heavily guarded secret The Tower held. Naturally the suspense made Jo's imagination run wickedly wild. "If he's even half as foxy as his voice is—"

"Stop drooling, Jo," Theresa admonished. "You're going to get saliva all over the seats, and they'll boot us back to coach."

Without a word Caylin reached over and unpaused the tape.

Killjoys, Jo thought, rolling her eyes. They're always obliterating my buzz!

"Once you go through baggage claim and customs at Heathrow," Uncle Sam continued, "you'll be met by a chauffeur holding this sign." The limo image was replaced with a shot of a cheesy-looking driver holding a handwritten sign reading Stevens. "That's it for now, ladies. Welcome to London . . . and good luck on your maiden mission."

As the screen faded to black, Jo removed her earphones and frowned in confusion. "Stevens?" she wondered aloud. "Who in the world is Stevens?"

Caylin pressed the fast-forward button, but there was nothing else on the tape. "That doesn't tell us anything!" she complained.

"I can't take this suspense much longer," Theresa moaned. "Those folks at The Tower *really* know how to lead a girl on, don't they?"

"Seriously," Jo murmured, her mind returning to the day she'd discovered that The Tower was not what she thought. She had been totally psyched about having an opportunity to see the world and do good things for the underprivileged—the kinds of things her father would have been proud to see her achieve. But that dream, like her father, had been killed in an instant.

Jo winced at the memory. She'd only been a high school freshman, sweet little Josefina Mercedes Carreras, the pride and joy of her father, who had defected from Cuba as a teenager and risen to prominence as one of Florida's most powerful judges. But then came that horrible day—the day Jo knew would haunt her for the rest of her life. Judge Victor Carreras had driven her to school and was just about to kiss her good-bye when shots rang out. He was gunned down by a vicious emissary from the drug cartel he had tried so hard to bring to justice.

An orphan at fourteen, Jo remembered, holding back tears. Her Brazilian-born mother had died during childbirth, so her father was the only family she had. Or so she'd thought until her aunt Thalia—her mother's sister—stepped into her life and brought Josefina to live in Miami with her and her husband, Enrique. Her newfound aunt and uncle took her on frequent trips to Brazil and introduced her to an extended family she never knew she had.

Still, the pain of losing her father was too great to bear. After she transferred to a new high school, she rejected good-little-girl Josefina and became fun-loving, boy-crazy Jo, connoisseur of fast food, faster fashion, and the fastest cars on earth. As hard as she tried to let go of her tragic past, it jumped up and bit her at the most inappropriate times—such as when The Tower informed her she was about to become a top secret international spy. She definitely wanted to fight for truth, justice, and the American way—her father had taught her well about that. Still, she couldn't help but fear that someday she would end up meeting the same senseless fate he had.

Suddenly the speaker above Jo's head crackled, breaking through her morose thoughts and shaking her back to reality. "We are beginning our final descent into London Heathrow," the captain announced. "Please fasten your seat belts. . . ."

Caylin immediately began following his orders. "Whoo-hoo!" she cheered. "It's about time!"

"I wonder what's in store for us when we touch down," Theresa mumbled, her gray eyes lost in thought.

"My feelings exactly," Jo said quietly as she gazed out the window at the clear blue sky. "One thing's for sure—our lives will never be the same again."

I *hate* baggage claim," Caylin groaned as she lugged her oversized bags toward customs. "My stuff is always the last to go by."

"They save the best for last," Theresa quipped.

"And now another line," Caylin moaned. "Waiting is the worst. *Especially* waiting for customs. I gotta be on the move."

"But look around! There's so much to see while we wait!" Jo said in excitement. "Everything here is so different—from the people to the clothes to the pay phones. This is just too incredible."

"As incredible as those customs boys, Jo?" Theresa asked, motioning to the two guys checking passports straight ahead.

Jo grinned. "Talk about hotties."

Caylin looked the guys up and down. "Yep, you could definitely fry an egg on them," she admitted. They looked maybe eighteen or nineteen and wore red button-down jackets with black slacks. Their short, neat dos were extra shiny, as if they had been heavily gelled recently. Basically the guys looked as if they belonged in a Brit-pop band—a band Caylin would have gladly put aside

15

her surfboard to see, no matter how tasty the waves were.

"Well, those guys are *way* too pale for my taste," Theresa said. "Haven't they ever heard of that blazing ball of fire in the sky—the *sun?*"

"We're in England, not the islands," Jo pointed out. "Pale boys with dark hair are always the flavor of the month here—except for that blond babe from Blur. But you'd never catch *him* under a sunlamp."

"That Damon is quite dashing," Theresa acquiesced. She leaned her head on Caylin's shoulder and made puppy eyes at the fellas. "Okay, second opinion. They *are* pretty cute."

Caylin shrugged Theresa off her shoulder playfully. "Take a chill pill," she murmured. "We're almost there."

"Passport?" Customs Boy No. 1 asked, his chestnut eyes boring into Caylin's own set of peepers.

"Sure," Caylin replied. As she handed over the navy blue booklet her fingers touched his for a millisecond, sending a shiver down her spine. She focused in on his shiny gold name tag: Ian. How beautifully British.

Ian opened the passport to the page with her vitals and squinted at the pic. "Length of stay?" he asked, stone-faced.

"Um, indefinite," she answered with a thousand-watt grin.

The corners of Ian's lips turned up slightly.

"Purpose of your visit?" he asked, meeting her gaze once again.

"To preserve world peace," she replied, deadpan. The second the words were out of her mouth, she heard Jo and Theresa stifling giggles behind her.

Ian chuckled. "No, seriously—what is the purpose of your visit?"

Caylin flipped her blond hair behind her shoulder flirtatiously. "Visiting my aunt . . . Stevens."

"Address while you're here?"

I have no idea, she realized. As she rolled her eyes up in cluelessness she decided to play off the move as if she had an airhead merit badge. "Um, me and my friends here, we're, like, staying in this hotel?" she replied in that statement-as-question tone she always found so grating.

"Which hotel is that, luv?" Ian asked, clearly amused.

"Oh, I can't *rememberrr*," she trilled. "My aunt, she's, like, out there somewhere?" She pointed past checkpoint security. "She's taking us there herself. I can get her if you—"

"No, that won't be necessary, miss," Ian replied. "Why aren't you staying with your aunt?"

"Well, she's kinda old. You know." Caylin rolled her eyes and feigned a yawn.

Ian winked and stamped her passport forcefully. "Very well, Miss Pike," he said. "Enjoy London."

Theresa handed over her passport with a coy smile. "If you're a good representation of the

17

male population, she'll have no prob enjoying your fair city."

As Ian gave Theresa the same drill, Caylin sighed with relief. The getting-the-aunt thing had been a gamble, but it had worked, just as Caylin knew it would. Guys never argue with an airhead, she thought. They crumble every time.

Caylin smiled as Theresa, through with her own private inquisition, did a quick brow sweep and came over to join her. She mouthed the words, That was close.

I know, Caylin mouthed back as she watched Jo begin to flirt wildly with Ian. But just when she thought they would all be home free, the words she'd been dreading to hear boomed throughout the checkpoint:

"*Would you please open this case for me, Miss Carreras?*"

"Why should I have to open a suitcase when no one else had to?" Jo complained, deeply horrified. The case Ian had singled out just happened to be the one holding a few key pieces of supersecret spy equipment supplied by The Tower. If Ian uncovers any of it, she realized, good old Scotland Yard will be called in to haul all three of us off to the hoosegow!

"Because this one is by far the bulkiest," Ian explained as he put the dreaded case on the metal table with a smile. "And if you have nothing to hide, you won't mind opening it. Right, luv?"

Your cuteness rating just dropped a million points, buddy, Jo thought angrily. She glanced over at Caylin and Theresa, who were both obviously doing their best not to freak.

"Listen," Jo seethed. "I put my blood, sweat, and *tears* into this packing job, okay? I stuffed so many clothes in this suitcase, it took, like, half an hour to zip the stupid thing up. So I'm warning you, if you open it . . . there's no guaranteeing you'll *ever* get it shut again."

Theresa gave a shaky laugh. "Yeah, she's right. I mean, the thing is so stuffed, I was afraid it would explode and blow up the whole plane!"

Jo felt as if her heart had just stopped dead. The rest of her body stock-still, she turned her head slowly in Theresa's direction. She felt as if she had turned into Robocop or something. In fact, she was almost certain that her head swivel and subsequent jaw drop were accompanied by a high-pitched robotic whine. Furious, she gave Theresa the end-all glare to end all end-all glares.

"Beg your pardon? Is—is that a joke?" Ian asked, the flat, lifeless note in his voice indicating just how hysterically *un*funny he found it.

Theresa noshed on her nails as if they were covered in chocolate. "Heh . . . sorry. Not funny."

"Indeed." Ian shook his head. "Well, I'll just have to have a look, then." He motioned for Jo to undo the locks.

Thanks a bunch, T., Jo thought with a gulp. She mentally crossed her fingers, praying Ian wouldn't find the shoe cam or the pressed powder compact phone too fishy.

As Ian shuffled through the bag someone behind Jo cleared his throat angrily. She snapped her head around in alarm but only saw a line of impatient, innocent-looking travelers, all checking their watches and shooting Jo dirty looks.

"Seems like the natives are getting restless," Caylin remarked as Ian picked up the shoe cam.

Ian didn't seem to notice Caylin *or* the beads of sweat forming at Jo's temples. He ran his fingers slowly over the shoe, turning every second into an hour. Jo's palms became swimming pools. Ian looked at the pump a beat longer— too long, Jo thought—before he quickly set it back atop the mound of mussed clothes. "Thanks, luv," he said, stamping her passport and motioning her past.

"That's *it?*" Jo cried.

Ian's perfect brow wrinkled. "How do you mean?" he asked suspiciously.

Whoops! "I mean . . . aren't you going to help me shut this thing?" Jo amended hastily as she mentally kicked herself in her Prada-clad behind.

"I can't be of assistance, I'm afraid, what with the queues and all," he apologized, managing to zip it up halfway. "But enjoy your stay."

"You can take *that* to the bank and cash it," Caylin quipped as she grabbed Jo with one hand and the half-closed bag with her other. "*Ta,* luv."

* * *

"I *cannot* believe we pulled that scam," Theresa exclaimed once she and her compatriots had sprinted far past the security checkpoint. "You two were awesome! I don't know what I would have done if any of that stuff happened to me."

"Well, it probably would have gone easier if you hadn't opened your big ol' mouth, Theresa," Jo said, glowering.

Theresa pouted. "Yeah, sorry . . . I was just trying to help, and—"

Jo shut her up with a little hug. "Hey, these things happen. I'm sorry I snapped at you like that. We made it, and that's what counts."

"Yeah—sometimes you just have to go with the flow," Caylin said as she completed the zip-up job on Jo's bag with a fierce final tug. "When you get in a tense situation, your body *and* your mind work in mysterious ways. It's just that *yours* were acting a little *extra* mysteriously."

"It'll never happen again, I swear!" Theresa crossed her heart and laughed. "Wow, you were so great, Jo. Your composure was so totally . . . composed."

Grinning, Jo blew on her fingernails and buffed them on her shoulder with a flourish. "I don't know what came over me, but whatever it was, it worked."

"You just used your womanly wiles on Ian," Theresa joked. "Admit it."

"Oh, I am *so* over him. 'Miss Carreras.' 'Thanks, luv.'" Jo gagged. "He practically treated me like a *criminal!* The only guy I'm concerned with at the moment is our limo driver."

Theresa opened her bag and took out her 35mm camera; she often used the powerful tele-photo lens as an impromptu, incognito telescope. She put the camera to her eye and scanned the crowd anxiously, her heart pounding when her lens lit on a sign reading Stevens. "I found him!" she ex-claimed, pointing to a tiny, shadowy figure in the distance.

"Let's hear it for the girl with the bionic eyes," Caylin cheered. "Come on!"

Her spirits back up and soaring, Theresa grabbed her bags and sprinted toward the limo driver. But an annoying voice in the back of her head kept re-minding her of her little screwup in customs. When it comes time for us to really shine, she thought, am I going to be the one who spills the darn polish?

The second Jo sank down into the soft leather seat in the back of the limousine, the door shut, the engine roared to life, and the black privacy screen went up. "Privacy, anyone?" she quipped.

At the sound of Jo's voice the TV in the back of the limo flickered on.

"Whoa!" Theresa enthused, jumping to check out the setup. She pointed to a tiny patch on the speaker. "Voice recognition mike," she explained. "Turns the whole shebang on."

Uncle Sam's voice filled the back of the limo.

"You've made it past customs," he intoned as a surveillance tape of Caylin putting on her air-head act for Ian came on-screen. "Just barely, I might add."

"How in the world did Uncle Sam manage that?" Caylin shrieked, her face flaming.

"No idea," Theresa squeaked, clearly flabber-gasted.

Jo's jaw dropped in disbelief. This spy stuff gets freakier every day, she realized. In fact, it's kinda creepy!

Caylin's image was replaced with a still of Buckingham Palace. "Welcome to London. Where you can shop till you drop at Harrods and Piccadilly Circus."

Jo's eyes lit up with excitement as different shops were shown, rapid-fire, on-screen. "Oooh," she breathed. "Maybe our mission is to masquerade as incurable shopaholics!"

That idea flew out the window as footage of a tall, ugly building began to roll. "This is the U.S. Embassy," Uncle Sam went on. "You'll be infiltrating the embassy, ladies. The mission ahead is deadly serious. The fate of the world depends on you."

Jo gulped. This was *not* quite what she had in mind for a maiden mission. She shot a glance at her partners, whose gazes were glued firmly to the thick limo carpet. We're all in this together, Jo thought, grabbing their hands in hers for strength. Theresa squeezed Jo's hand in response. Caylin met her gaze and nodded in agreement, as if she had read Jo's mind.

"Watch carefully," Uncle Sam continued. "The next face you will see belongs to William Nicholson, the American ambassador to the U.K."

The image of a ruggedly handsome man in his late fifties filled the screen. Caylin scooted up in her seat and narrowed her eyes as if she were drinking in every line on Nicholson's time-worn face.

"Nicholson is a former media mogul," Uncle Sam told them. "Born in America, he graduated from Oxford and soon gained ownership of several newspapers in the U.S. and U.K., as well as a British radio franchise and an American television network. He gave it all up for a life of politics—his countless media outlets and British education helped him earn an ambassadorship to the U.K. The next face you see belongs to his son, Jonathon."

Theresa gulped.

Caylin gasped.

Jo grinned. The tall, dark, and handsome image that was now gracing the screen had cheekbones for years, shoulders for miles, and thick, dark eyelashes for days. Jonathon Nicholson's brown eyes seemed to gaze lovingly into Jo's right through the TV, and the glow coming off his Colgate smile was most certainly *not* provided by electricity. Jo rubbed her hands together in anticipation of having a superfox like Jonathon working on the Spy

Girls' side—or better yet, right by her-and-*only*-her side.

"Jonathon Nicholson is nineteen years old," Uncle Sam began, his tone ominous. "Born and raised in America, he, like his father, is being schooled at Oxford. However, last week Jonathon took leave from his studies with no explanation, winding up in the service of his father at the embassy. The Tower has reason to believe this event is linked to the murder of Special Agent Frank Devaroux, who was found dead on the embassy grounds almost simultaneously."

Jo's giddy excitement whooshed out of her like air out of a balloon. Her blood chilled instantly.

"Dead?" Theresa squealed.

"Jonathon is our primary suspect," Uncle Sam announced.

"But look at that gorgeous face," Caylin lamented. "How could Jonathon possibly be involved with icing an agent?"

"Looks can be deceiving," Jo said flatly. The man who had killed her father might have looked like James Dean, but he had the heart of Charles Manson. Correction, Jo thought. He had no heart at all.

As Jonathon's picture was replaced by a hazy one of a smiling Special Agent Devaroux, Jo instantly wished she could take back all the hormonally hysterical thoughts she'd had about the creep who had more than likely killed him. I bet Agent Devaroux never knew what hit him, Jo thought, an image of her father's face flashing across her mind. Well, once I set my sights on Jonathon Nicholson, he'll never know, either!

Caylin studied the face of Special Agent Devaroux, her heart pumping—with excitement or dread, she couldn't tell. But she ignored her heart-beat and perked up her ears when Uncle Sam continued his narration.

"After the Soviet Union broke up, a great number of nuclear warheads went unaccounted for," he began. "A rumor has been floating around that a complete list of these purloined nuclear weapons—along with their exact locations—exists and has been hidden away somewhere in Europe. Special Agent Devaroux had narrowed the location down to the U.S. Embassy in London, but as far as we know, he got no further."

"I'll say," Theresa whispered.

"The Tower has reason to believe that Jonathon Nicholson is working with terrorist forces to acquire this list," Uncle Sam went on. "The timing of Devaroux's death, so close to Jonathon's sudden arrival at the embassy, only serves to bolster this belief. If Jonathon and his terrorist allies are successful, the list could be used to jeopardize world safety. That is why the three of you are assigned to gather information about Jonathon's daily activities, his partners in crime, and what you believe to be his motivations and report back with them on a daily basis."

As Jonathon's picture reappeared on-screen, Caylin whistled. "For a bad guy he sure is looking *gooooood!*"

"He's hotter than Arizona in July," Theresa agreed, fanning herself. "You should have no problem tailing *him*, Jo," she joked. To Caylin's utter surprise, Jo remained silent and tight-lipped. She was about to check Jo for a pulse when Uncle Sam's voice-over started again.

"From this moment forward," he said gravely, "you will learn things on a need-to-know basis. You'll soon arrive at the Ritz hotel on Piccadilly. Once there, check in under the name Camilla Stevens. The desk staff has been prepped to receive you and take you immediately to your suite, which will serve as your base of operations for the duration of your mission. You'll find further information in the suite's safe, combination thirty-six, twenty-four, thirty-six."

"Barbie's measurements!" Theresa joked as Jo scribbled the info on her hand.

The screen went black, sending Caylin into a total adrenaline rush. Now that she knew the scoop, she felt light-headed enough to float straight through the limo's sunroof. "This is it," she whispered, her eyes shining with joy as she gazed at her two partners—and friends—for life. "It's finally happening. We're real Spy Girls now!"

Whoa, this is heaven!" Jo exclaimed as she entered the busy lobby of the Ritz. Her jaw dropped as she took in the thick Turkish carpets, the ornate chandeliers, the bouquets of flowers that seemed to be everywhere.

Caylin twirled around gleefully. "I'll say."

"It sure beats Motel Six," joked Theresa, smirking. "Okay, so what's the name we're supposed to check in under?"

"I wrote it on my hand—hold on," Jo said, dropping her luggage and bringing her palm to her face. "It's—oh no! My suitcase handle must have rubbed it off. I can't read *what* it says."

Caylin moaned. "I remember the Stevens part, but that's it. Now what are we supposed to do?"

"Don't panic," Theresa said calmly. "Let's just think for a second. Wasn't it Clarissa?"

"No, that's Sabrina the Teenage Witch's old show—you know, *Clarissa Explains It All,*" Jo said.

"Well, if we can't remember the name, maybe we can get *her* to explain it all to Uncle Sam," Caylin said. "The name definitely started with a *C*.

29

And I think it had something to do with Prince Charles." Caylin squinted. "What's his girlfriend's name? Carlotta?"

"Camilla!" Jo said triumphantly.

"You rock," Theresa cheered as she followed Jo to the front desk. "Let's hope our room does as well."

While Jo told the front desk clerk their alias, Theresa held her breath and crossed her fingers behind her back for good luck. It must have worked because they were all given card keys with no hassles despite the fact that they had no IDs whatsoever bearing the name of Camilla Stevens. Uncle Sam obviously has our back, Theresa thought thankfully, her heart rate slowing down to normal.

As the porter was called to fetch their bags Theresa gazed around the opulent lobby. She felt as if she were in one bigger-than-life dream. Here she was in London at the swankiest hotel in town, representing the U.S. government! It seemed too good to be true. So good that she floated all the way to the elevator, nearly ramming into a woman who was entering at the same time.

"Oops, sorry," she said, giving the lady an apologetic grin.

The woman gave her a cold smile and a brisk nod. Something in her eyes sent shivers up Theresa's spine. The whole way up to the fourteenth floor the woman seemed to be watching her every move. Theresa didn't like that one bit. She took note of the woman's features just in case. Early thirties. Tall and thin. Short, dark hair. Porcelain skin. Full lips—probably collagen enhanced. Looked like she could have played the vixen on *Melrose Place* or something.

The woman's cold, dead stare was giving Theresa the definite creeps. How can I wipe that look off her face? she wondered, suddenly getting an idea. Still holding her gaze, Theresa casually dropped her not-so-light backpack right on the woman's foot. Theresa's blood chilled instantly—the woman's gaze was unwavering and unchanged. She didn't blink; she didn't move. After a few unbearable seconds Theresa shamefacedly picked up her backpack and stared straight ahead. This woman was *definitely* bad news.

As they reached the fourteenth floor the woman gave them one last searching gaze as they exited the elevator. After the doors closed, Theresa waved Jo and Caylin back for a miniconference while the porter continued on toward 1423. "Did you guys notice that short-haired chick?" she whispered. "She was totally evil."

"Well, I *did* like her hair," Jo said lightly. "I wish I could pull off the short-hair look. It's so glam."

"Hardly!" Theresa wrinkled her nose in disgust. "Anyway, her do is the least of my concerns. My gut tells me she's up to no good."

*　　*　　*

Caylin's heart raced as she set foot in 1423, the *sweetest* suite she had ever seen. "Not too shabby," she murmured with a satisfied nod. Growing up the child of wealthy, globe-trotting parents, Caylin was used to staying at five-star hotels. But staying in one without parental supervision felt way beyond supercool.

Jo shrieked with delight. "Whoa, can we say *superglam?*" She ran over to the baby grand in the middle of the room and began bashing out "Chopsticks."

"Check out the sound system!" Theresa cried, eyeing the speakers mounted discreetly in the ceiling.

"Glad it meets your approval," the porter said as he began leading Caylin on a tour of the three-bedroom suite. He started with the three bedrooms, each door adorned with a sign displaying each of their names. The bedrooms were amazing—with huge, pillow-covered four-poster beds, beautiful oak dressers, candles everywhere, TVs and VCRs, and antique desks complete with personal phones, fax machines, and laptop computers.

Theresa skipped merrily into her bedroom. "I could *definitely* call this place home," she breathed.

"I'll say," Caylin agreed. She'd secretly had nightmares of staying in some roach-infested dump of a hostel during their mission, so these surroundings were all the more welcome. Although Caylin was all for roughing it if necessary, part of her still loved the plush life.

As the porter continued the tour through the

two huge bathrooms, dominated by pink marble fixtures and huge, Jacuzzi-style bathtubs, Jo exclaimed, "Dibs!"

"Can I just live here forever?" Theresa asked as the porter led them all toward the minibar, which was specially stocked with nothing but diet Coke, cranberry juice, and Evian.

"Our faves!" Caylin said, reaching for a bottled water. "I feel like Fiona Apple or something. You know how rock stars always request weird stuff to eat backstage, like M&M's with no brown ones? We have our demands, too."

"Just don't ask me to sing—that could be brutal," Theresa said with a chuckle.

"For real," Jo said. "I've heard her sing along to her Walkman, and Jewel she's not."

Jo and Theresa's ribbing was cut short when the porter showed them the safe, where they knew Uncle Sam's top secret info was awaiting them. Caylin could barely contain her anticipation as he explained the importance of placing valuables in there.

We've already *got* something valuable in there, she thought impatiently as she silently willed the guy to speed up his spiel. As soon as he paused to take a breath Caylin immediately tipped him five pounds—"the amount I'd like to lose before Christmas," Theresa quipped—before she shooed him out the door. She could hardly wait to see what juicy details were hidden behind that silver, combination-locked door.

* * *

"'You are to report to the American Embassy at nine A.M. sharp tomorrow morning, Wednesday, separately,'" Theresa, parked on the velvet couch in front of the baby grand, read aloud from the confidential Tower fax Caylin had rescued from the safe. Her hands trembled slightly over the importance of what she was reading. This fax was going to change their lives forever!

"'Jo will be a personal translator known as *Natascia Sanchez*,'" Theresa continued. "'Brazil born, America raised, currently on a work visa for six months. This position will allow her to be privy to sensitive information.'"

"Natascia Sanchez?" Jo said, laughing. "What am I, a salsa singer or something? That name is so cheesy, I could make nachos with it."

Theresa cracked up. "Okay, what's next. . . . 'Caylin will be'—*no way!*—'a housekeeper from Camden Town, London, since most of the housekeepers are locals,'" Theresa recited, noticing Caylin's falling features. "'Her alias is *Louise Browning*. In this capacity she can snoop through the trash and bug offices without suspicion.' And use that fabulous accent, too, I might add."

Caylin's jaw dropped. "That *must* be a misprint!" she cried, snatching the fax out of Theresa's hands. "I've had a few housekeepers, but that doesn't qualify me to *be* one. Hello, where's the action? Where's the adventure?"

"It won't be *that* horrible," Theresa lied, reclaiming

the fax. "And you might not even have to do windows—who knows."

"And maybe you'll get to wear one of those cute black-and-white outfits!" Jo exclaimed.

"Oh, puh-*leeze*," Caylin complained.

Theresa cleared her throat impatiently, dying to find out her own assignment. "'Theresa,'" she continued, "'will be an American call-forwarding technician known as *Emma Webster*. This will allow her to track who's getting calls from whom.' All right!"

"Wanna trade?" Caylin asked hopefully.

"No way, José," Theresa replied as she silently thanked her lucky stars. "I'm not trading a phone for a feather duster. Sorry."

"What else does the letter say?" Jo asked. "Anything about a set of wheels in there?"

"Unfortunately for you, no," Theresa said. "But there is stuff about where we need to go, who we need to report to." Theresa skimmed the page with her index finger. "Hey, get this: 'Appropriate wardrobe is already in your closets. Good luck!'"

The moment Theresa uttered the word *wardrobe*, Jo yelped and jumped to her feet. "Let's go!"

Jo and Caylin hightailed it to their respective closets while Theresa lagged behind.

"We are so stylin'!" Jo yelled. She ran out of her room, her arms laden with ultrahip office wear.

"Stylin' *and* profilin'," Caylin exclaimed. She stood at her closet, pushing aside her drab gray housekeeper's dresses to reveal totally awesome Jean Paul Gaultier clubbing clothes. "Wow, I guess British housekeepers lead pretty wild nightlives."

Theresa walked into her room, opened her closet, and picked over her new duds with disdain. "I could pretty much take or leave this stuff."

Caylin wandered into Theresa's room, followed by Jo, who was showing off an ultraglam lime green suit. "Check out the new me!" she cheered, spinning around with the suit held tightly to her bod.

"I don't see how you get so worked up over what's essentially just a piece of material and some thread," Theresa said, rolling her eyes.

Caylin laughed. "For the daughter of a fashion designer, you sure don't like clothes very much."

"That's precisely why she *doesn't* like fashion," Jo declared. "Can we say, *rebellion* against the 'rents?"

Theresa shook her head even though Jo's statement was pretty much on the money. "At least I'm not a fashion junkie like *some* people I know," she said with a smile.

"Guilty as charged," Jo announced, whirling around once more.

"This is all so hard to believe," Caylin said as she shrugged off a funky fake fur pea coat. "Here we are, real international spies about to embark on our first mission. And only four months ago we arrived at The Tower, totally clueless."

"I thought it was a scam when I found out the truth about The Tower," Jo recalled.

"Remember how they told us there would be seventeen people on our 'outreach mission'?" Theresa asked, laughing.

"Not told," Jo replied. "*Lied.*"

When Theresa realized that only she, Caylin, and Jo had shown up for "active duty," she had begun to wonder if she had made a massive mistake. After all, she'd put off her early enrollment bid at the University of Chicago for what she thought would be an opportunity to put her technological prowess to good use, perhaps to help the Russian population learn job-worthy computer skills.

But that night all her questions had been answered during a top secret meeting about her true calling: to protect and serve the world on missions where a seventeen- or eighteen-year-old girl would be appropriate and/or the least likely to be suspected. The whole seventeen-member-outreach-mission thing had been a ruse concocted to keep her and her two new partners from walking out of The Tower *tout de suite*.

"It took some convincing for me to believe The Tower was legit," Theresa recalled. "But once convinced, I realized I was up to the challenge."

Are you really? a little voice in her head asked. She pushed it aside quickly. She'd made it this far, after all. It was too late to talk herself out of her decision now.

After a long, refreshing shower Caylin wrapped herself in the lush terry bathrobe provided by the

Ritz, towel-dried her shoulder-length blond hair, and padded out into the living room of the suite, where Theresa was hooking up her laptop and Jo was gabbing on the phone in Portuguese—probably to her aunt. Quietly Caylin picked up the fax from The Tower and looked it over one last time to be absolutely sure she had the specifics of her mission straight before she went to bed.

She couldn't wait for the morning to come. Patience, to Caylin, was hardly a virtue—and the same went for sitting still. The first week of security training at The Tower had been held in a classroom, and Caylin had wanted to pull her hair out. If she had wanted to be trapped in a classroom all day, she would have gone to UC Berkeley, where she could have surfed and swam and actually had a life. She started to think The Tower was total Snoozeville—until the real fun began. In addition to the training in concocting disguises and learning accents there had been kickboxing, skydiving, motorcycle racing—you name it. She'd even learned yoga, which had helped her to channel her impatient energies toward a more productive goal.

Her nerves jangling and her muscles aching to move, Caylin put the fax aside and sat on the floor in the lotus position. She closed her eyes, stretched her arms above her head, and arched her back, willing the tension in her body to work its way up and out of her. When she opened her eyes, she saw that Theresa had planted herself on the floor next to her and was doing the same thing.

"Helps, doesn't it?" Caylin asked.

Theresa exhaled and smiled. "Totally. The whole physical part of our training was so brutal for me," she confessed. "I felt like I was in sixth-grade gym class again. You know, always last to be picked for the team. Stick me in a tae kwon do class and I feel worthless."

Caylin widened her eyes, genuinely shocked. "I always thought you really rocked as an athlete."

"Really?"

"Me too," Jo added, coming over to join them after her phone session. "You didn't seem entirely into it or anything at first, but you definitely rip."

"Me? Rip?" Theresa laughed. "It's so funny when you find out what people think of you—it's usually so *not* what you think of yourself."

"Totally. I mean, what'd you guys think of *me* at first?" Caylin asked excitedly.

"I have to admit, my first impression was that you were a prima donna," Theresa confessed. "But I think that's because of your Barbie-perfect looks. Once I got to know you, I realized you were down-to-earth and totally not like that."

"Same here," Jo admitted. "I thought you'd be way stuck-up, but you ended up being a total doll. No offense."

"None taken—I'm used to it," Caylin said. "Everyone always leans on the whole princess thing. I guess it's the hair."

Theresa laughed. "So . . . what was your first impression of me?"

Caylin scratched her forehead thoughtfully. "A

very smart and together girl who needs to cut loose every once in a while."

"I totally thought you were some elitist girl genius," Jo admitted. "But that was probably because you had your nose buried in a book the first few hours after I met you."

Theresa shrugged. "I was bored. With all that waiting around for those fourteen invisible others, I had to entertain myself *somehow.*"

"Well, what about me?" Jo asked mischievously. "Come on, hit me with your best shot!"

"I thought you were totally worldly," Caylin recalled. "Been everywhere, seen everything—that type of girl."

"Me too," Theresa chimed in. "I immediately picked up on how confident, dynamic, and pretty much unshakable you are."

"Thanks—but I'm not always unshakable," Jo confessed. "Especially around gorgeous guys. Hotties are my weakness."

"Speaking of hot, what about Jonathon Nicholson?" Theresa asked. "I know he's the main focus of our investigation, but can we say *cute?*"

"Aw yeah!" Caylin exclaimed.

"Murderers are *not* hot in my book," Jo stated angrily. And to Caylin's shock, she stood up, walked to her bedroom, and slammed the door.

"Jo? Are you okay?"

"If you don't let us in, Jo, I'm going to break this door down! I mean it!"

"I'm sure you do, Cay," Jo mumbled to herself as she lifted her tear-streaked face from the pillow. Theresa and Caylin had been pounding on the door for five minutes straight now, and the noise was hardly doing anything to make her feel better. She wiped her eyes on the corner of a pillowcase, leaving two dark mascara smears, but she didn't care. She just wanted to put the traumas of her past behind her. Why did that seem so impossible?

The moment she unlocked the door, she was wrapped in a massive group bear hug.

"Oh, Jo, we're so sorry," Theresa cried. "That was really insensitive of us—we didn't mean to hurt your feelings, honest."

"It totally slipped my mind about your father," Caylin added, squeezing Jo tighter. "I should have realized when you got so quiet in the limo today that was what you were thinking about. It was so stupid of me."

"Me too," Theresa agreed.

Sniffling, Jo stepped out of the hug and smiled weakly. "It's okay," she said quietly. "It's just that all this talk about starting at The Tower and knowing that our first big mission is about to begin—it's bringing up a lot of bad memories. I shouldn't let myself get so upset about this kind of stuff . . . because I'm going to have to deal with it all the time from now on."

"I can't imagine what you're going through," Caylin said, shaking her head sadly. "Do you want to talk about it?"

"Thanks . . . no," Jo replied. "I should just go to bed. I'm pretty worn-out, I guess."

Theresa looked at her watch. "You're right—it's seven o'clock here, so it's one in the afternoon back in D.C. And we sure didn't get much sleep on the red-eye over."

"Yeah, I guess we're all a little jet-lagged," Caylin observed. "We'd better turn in so we can be fresh as daisies for our first big day."

After they'd all said their good nights, Jo smiled, thankful that her friends hadn't pressed her to discuss her father. Some people thought Jo should talk about him, as if she could get rid of the pain by hashing out the ugly details for the umpteenth time. But Caylin and Theresa seemed to understand that sometimes Jo didn't want group therapy.

She'd convinced herself that becoming a spy would be the best way for her to get over the death of her father once and for all. But she couldn't help wondering if spending the rest of her life investigating and, hopefully, *preventing* nothing *but* death—of people, of truth, of justice—was just going to make it all the more difficult.

She changed into her boxers and her old Luis Miguel T-shirt—a souvenir from the first concert her father had ever taken her to—and sat down on her bed. I'm not doing this to forget my father, she reminded herself. I'm doing this to keep his memory alive. There. With a smile on her face and an image of Victor Carreras in her mind, Jo knew she was ready.

I t's a jolly good morning, I say," Caylin remarked on the three-block walk to the embassy on a bright and sunny Wednesday morning.

"With an accent like that, even *I'm* starting to buy that you're a Brit," Jo remarked as they walked past row house upon row house—council flats, as they were known in Brit parlance—along the narrow, winding road. Even though she spoke four languages fluently, Jo had experienced a few difficulties trying to perfect the accent herself; hence her *Americanista* status on the mission. Obviously Caylin didn't have the same problem.

"Before you know it, Cay, you'll be drinking tea with clotted cream and eating scones at every meal," Theresa joked. "And then all the color will magically drain out of your skin."

"Yeah, that sun-kissed look doesn't quite match your accent," Jo said, catching their reflection in a store window. What she saw staring back at her in the streaked glass was Caylin, a striking blond in an *un*striking gray housecoat; Theresa, a brunette beauty in a simple cotton sundress; and herself, an exotic, out-of-place-looking chick dressed to the nines in a black business suit. They all looked pretty darn good in Jo's eyes.

"Hey, we'd better split up," Theresa suggested. "The embassy's only a block away."

"Consider it done," Caylin said, initiating a good-luck high five. As their hands slapped together Jo, Caylin, and Theresa disappeared, leaving Natascia, Louise, and Emma to take their places.

"Emma Webster to see Ms. Dalton, the voice mail manager," Theresa told the receptionist nervously. She repeated her pseudonym over and over in her mind like a mantra—Emma Webster, Emma Webster, Emma Webster—and prayed she wouldn't blow her cover in front of her new boss.

"Let me check," said the polished redhead, motioning for Theresa to have a seat on the nearest couch. As Theresa parked it she studied her new surroundings. The large, airy lobby had the feel of a government agency but with more class and cash than those she'd had to deal with back home as a Tower trainee. The couches were leather rather than vinyl, and the art on the walls was actually quite attractive. She was so absorbed, she nearly jumped out of her skin when the receptionist called her new name loudly.

"Yes?" Theresa asked, startled.

"Ms. Dalton can see you now, Ms. Webster," the receptionist announced. "Down that hall, third door on the left."

"Thank you." Theresa stood up and smoothed

her sundress. Walking down the narrow hall, she held on to her composure. She had trained four long months for this moment. She was ready. Or better yet, Emma Webster was ready.

As she walked in the office marked Nora Dalton, Theresa's heart sank. Behind the immaculate desk sat a woman with a severe silver bun and a gray suit to match. Not exactly the kind of boss who'd let the good times roll, she thought, plastering a smile on her face to mask her disappointment.

"Hello, Ms. Dalton? I'm Emma. Emma Webster," she said in a rock solid voice, sticking her hand out for the obligatory nice-to-meet-you handshake.

"Hello, Ms. Webster," Ms. Dalton said, looking her up and down with seeming disdain. "Have a seat."

As Theresa sank into the brown leather chair her spirits sank with her. By the sour expression on Ms. Dalton's face, it didn't look as if she was too keen on her *or* her casual attire.

"You've come highly recommended for the job of voice mail technician," Ms. Dalton began, "but I'd like to discuss your credentials. Could you explain to me why you feel you're qualified for the position?"

Theresa was totally confused. Didn't she already *have* the position? "Um, well . . . I just *love* telephones, and my grandmother was a switchboard operator way back when, so I guess the passion runs in the family."

Ms. Dalton looked at her suspiciously. Was the grandmother bit too much? Theresa wondered. "And, uh," she continued nervously, "at my last job there were fifty lines that were lit up all the time."

"Your last job?" Ms. Dalton asked, looking down at a piece of paper in front of her. "Which job was that?"

Theresa took a deep breath. "Well, I was the voice mail technician for Bill Gates—you know, the president of Microsoft? And since he's one of the richest men in America, the phone was always ringing off the hook. I was forwarding calls, screening calls, placing calls, patching people through to his car phone . . . the whole nine yards."

Ms. Dalton's eyes lit up. "Well, that's most impressive. To have gone from working for Sam Walton to Bill Gates!"

"Um, Sam Walton?" Theresa asked, trying to disguise her confusion.

"Yes, how delightful to have had the founder of Wal-Mart as an uncle," she said, clasping her hands. "Your reference mentions you and your uncle Sam were quite close."

A lightbulb clicked on inside Theresa's head. Uncle Sam! It would have been nice of him to let her know the details of her resume. "Well, yes, we were," Theresa said solemnly. "May he rest in peace."

Ms. Dalton's features softened. "His memory will live on with every call you answer here at the

46

embassy, I assure you." She rose from her chair. "Follow me, Ms. Webster. I'll teach you all you need to know."

As she trailed Ms. Dalton out the door Theresa breathed a deep sigh of relief and gave herself a mental pat on the back. Snow job one—successful!

"Mr. Nicholson, I'd like to introduce you to our newest translator," Sandra Frankel, Jo's *very* blond and British boss, announced as she led Jo into a posh office where none other than William Nicholson stood up from behind his desk and smiled welcomingly.

Jo gave Mr. Nicholson her best I-know-you-but-I-*don't*-know-you look, certain that her face showed no signs of recognition. "Nice to meet you," she said confidently, extending her arm to offer a handshake. "I'm Jo—uh, *jovial* to be here. Natascia. Natascia Sanchez."

Jo panicked momentarily, hoping Mr. Nicholson didn't notice her slipup. But to her relief, he shook her hand without missing a beat. "Nice to meet you, Natascia," he said, flashing a pearly white grin. "William Nicholson."

Sandra, also seemingly oblivious to Jo's flub, quickly reeled off Jo's extensive credentials: fluent in Spanish, French, and Portuguese; lived in Cuba, Mexico, and Brazil; degree in international relations. Everything but the language and Brazil parts were fabricated, but Jo smiled proudly as if every word were the honest truth.

"Well, I'm impressed," Mr. Nicholson said, nodding enthusiastically. "So accomplished for such a young girl. How old are you?"

"Twenty-one," Jo lied.

"I have a son about your age," Mr. Nicholson said. "He's interning here for the summer, so I'm sure you'll meet him one of these days. At any rate, Ms. Sanchez, we're pleased to have you on board."

"She'll be on call for you whenever you need her, sir," Sandra said. "When she's not working for you, she'll be translating the documents for the conference."

Mr. Nicholson nodded thoughtfully. "Good, good. That conference is creeping up on us, isn't it? Just a few weeks away."

"Yes, sir," Sandra chirped.

What conference? Jo wondered. She vowed to get the dirt as soon as possible.

"Well, I'm sure I'll see you soon, Ms. Sanchez," Mr. Nicholson said hastily. "Thanks for bringing her by, Ms. Frankel."

Sandra shook his hand forcefully. "Very good, sir."

"See you soon," Jo called, wiggling her fingers in good-bye.

As she followed Sandra out, Jo breathed a sigh of relief. Other than almost completely blowing her cover, things didn't go too badly at all.

"That went well," Sandra whispered, leading Jo down the fluorescent-lit hall. "Mr. Nicholson is really nice to work with. Very polite."

Jo nodded. "He seemed really sweet. What's the conference you two were talking about?"

"Oh, the World Peace Conference," Sandra said. "It's this really grand affair we're hosting two weeks from next Monday, and anyone who's anyone in politics will be there. Following the conference will be a formal ball. As a translator, you'll be invited."

"Great!" Jo exclaimed. "It sounds totally glamorous. But I'm sure there's a lot to be done before then."

"You don't know the half of it," Sandra said. "I'm running around like a chicken with my head cut off trying to get all the documents translated. But I'm sure it will all work out."

"Absolutely," Jo assured her. "I'll do everything I can to help."

"Well, I appreciate that," Sandra replied. "Actually, it'd be brilliant if you could help pick out some of the music to be played at the ball after the conference. We need some . . . you know . . . *up-tempo* numbers, and I'm hardly one to judge."

"I'd love to! Just say the word."

"Well, we've got a while to go yet, but I'll let you know." Sandra cleared her throat. "And now it's time to meet the rest of the translators." She led Jo into the large translation department. It consisted of several cubicles—one for each of the translators—and private offices for Sandra and her second in command. Enormous file cabinets lined the walls.

"This is Natascia Sanchez, our newest translator,"

Sandra announced. "Natascia, meet Flora, Nakita, Franz, Julius, Nana, and Antonio."

While Sandra rattled on about her "credentials," Jo made an effort to remember her new coworkers: Flora, a serious-looking woman with dark hair and glasses; Nakita, a Nordic blond girl around Jo's age; Franz, a pale brunette hipster boy; Julius, a distinguished man with salt-and-pepper hair and beard; Nana, an older woman with short red hair tucked under a black beret; Antonio—*whoa!* Jo almost seriously lost it when she laid eyes on him. Early twenties, dark hair, olive skin . . . *ouch!*

"It's great to meet you all," Jo said, directing this comment to Antonio in particular. *You are utterly amazing,* she told him silently, hoping her open admiration was beaming out through her ebony eyes. *Like Antonio Sabato Jr. times ten!* When Antonio held her gaze a beat too long, her heart sped up to about a million miles an hour. Was she having the same effect on him?

After everyone waved and welcomed her to the group, Sandra whisked her away for a tour of the embassy. First stop: the ballroom where the World Peace Conference was to be held. It was a massive, opulent room, with shining wood floors and luxurious patterned carpets. A huge chandelier dominated the space, creating an atmosphere of Old World elegance.

"This is incredible," Jo cooed.

"It *is* smashing," Sandra agreed. "And will be even more so when it's filled with the most important people in the world. Let me show you back to the office, where some of the old files are archived."

As Jo followed Sandra back to the far corner of the room she noticed a door marked Private next to the ladies' room.

"Uh, Sandra," she asked, curiosity piqued, "would you excuse me while I go to the little girls' room?"

Sandra grinned. "Oh, sure, the loo's right there. I'll be in that office straight ahead."

"Okay," Jo said, ducking into the bathroom. After a few moments she poked her head out to make sure the coast was clear, then slid over to the mystery door. As Jo twisted the knob to the right her pulse raced. But her heart soon sank like the *Titanic* as she realized the knob wasn't budging. *Locked!*

"Not that door, Natascia."

Jo jumped and whirled around to see Sandra peeking around the office door. She gulped, her heart pounding madly. Caught red-handed!

"Here." Sandra met her out in the hall and directed Jo toward the ladies' room door. "*This* one."

Jo hit her forehead with her hand, relieved that Sandra hadn't busted her. "Duh!" she exclaimed. "Sometimes I am *such* an airhead."

She walked back into the bathroom to check her lipstick, but all the while her mind was spinning. Just what was behind that locked door that was so private? If Sandra's cool response is any indication, she decided, maybe it's nothing at all.

* * *

Caylin ran her feather duster along a smooth oak desk, her mind wandering in a thousand directions. Why did *she* have to be the one assigned to be the maid? The only perk of the job thus far was that she got to use an accent. Too bad she didn't have anyone to use it on. Her boss had talked to her for thirty seconds, tops—long enough to hand her a bucket of cleaning supplies and a garbage can and to tell her which offices she was in charge of cleaning.

Twenty offices, six conference rooms, and two suites would be spic and span thanks to Caylin's services by day's end, according to Fiona, a frizzy-haired, twentysomething woman who also happened to be Caylin's boss. Fiona had quickly bailed, leaving Caylin alone with her thoughts. And those thoughts were none too sweet at the moment, considering most offices were empty—their inhabitants in meetings—and the few people she had encountered had avoided her gaze, not even saying so much as hello. Caylin was used to being a center-of-attention fly girl, not an ignored fly on the wall. And now, with each office she cleaned, her mood grew more and more sour.

"Cor blimey!" Caylin shrieked as something seeped down her dress during a routine garbage removal. After some close inspection she discovered that an open soda can at the top of the overflowing trash bag was obviously the culprit.

"What a blazing idiot," she cursed the absent office inhabitant while staring at a smiling family portrait on his desk. People who leave open Coke cans in trash cans don't deserve to smile, she thought, barely resisting the urge to smash its frame to bits. During training at The Tower she had been taught that a lot could be learned about a person by going through his or her trash. It sure sounded good in theory, but actually *doing* it was another matter entirely. Basically all she'd learned so far was that the bigwigs at the U.S. Embassy had a taste for junk food and a distaste for junk mail.

As she stormed out of the office and started down the hall Caylin took a deep breath. "Keep your eyes on the prize, *Louise*," she told her alter ego. The suites, where Jonathon Nicholson hopefully lived, were her next stop.

Snooping through Jonathon's garbage will make up for all this other . . . uh, garbage, she assured herself. Her pulse raced as she got closer and closer to the door. Will he be behind it? she wondered. The possibility gave her a thrilling rush.

She reached the door of the mystery suite, opened the lock easily with her all-access service key, and placed a trembling hand on the knob. Breath held in anticipation, she hastily pushed open the door, unable to stand the suspense a moment longer. She was dying to know what—or who—lay in wait on the other side.

"So Jonathon wasn't even *there*," Caylin complained to Uncle Sam's silhouette via videophone that evening. "After my bore of a day I thought his suite would be pay dirt. But it was practically empty—just a few shirts, a pair of pants, and that's it. Anticlimactic, to say the least."

"Well, I've got some scoop," Jo piped up. "I met William Nicholson through Sandra, the translator coordinator. It was your typical meet-and-greet, no biggie. But he did mention that I'd be meeting Jonathon 'one of these days.'"

"If Jonathon's father said that and Jonathon's suite is practically empty, then he must be out of town," Theresa deduced. "His name came up a lot in the call-forwarding area at the embassy today. Everyone in the department was told to take messages for him—and he gets a *lot* of calls. I asked around about where he could be, but no one in the department had a clue."

"Keep your eyes and ears open," Uncle Sam instructed. "Anything else to report?"

"There's this World Peace Conference coming up, and it sounds like it's going to be major," Jo said.

"It's about time you mentioned that," Uncle Sam remarked.

"What do you mean?" Theresa's brow wrinkled in thought. "Oh, I get it. You didn't tell us about the conference because you wanted us to find out about it ourselves. Just like you didn't tell me about my faked credential working for my 'uncle' Sam Walton!"

Uncle Sam chuckled. "That was quite clever, I thought."

"Oh, please!" Theresa cried. "That joke was so lame, even Carrot Top wouldn't touch it."

"All right, all right, let's deep-six this discussion," Caylin demanded with a wave of her hand. "We've got more important things to think about—like how this race for the list of nuclear warheads is timed to coincide with the conference."

"Exactly," Uncle Sam replied. "Now grab a pen, Caylin. I've got an assignment for you."

Caylin jumped up and retrieved a pen from the antique desk in the corner of the room. "Okay, Uncle Sam, shoot."

"You will go to the first-floor bathroom in the embassy," he commanded. "There will be eight bugs in the sanitary napkin machine, hidden in a tampon."

A tampon? Caylin thought, looking at Jo and Theresa in horror.

"Then you are to take those and place four in Jonathon's suite and four in William's suite," he continued. "The offices we'll do later since that will be a bit riskier and take some more planning. Any questions?"

Caylin looked up from the notes she'd been scrawling furiously and grinned, her grossed-out look replaced with one of delicious anticipation. "Nope, I got it," she said. "Four bugs each, and we're not talking about the ones you could kill with Raid."

Uncle Sam's silhouette nodded. "Okay, Theresa, you're next."

"Pass that pen over, Cay," Theresa requested

gleefully. She caught it in midair and looked directly into the video cam. "Okay, Uncle Sam, give me the news."

"Will do, Theresa," Uncle Sam said. "You're to record all calls William and Jonathon receive—time, date, from whom—into your tape recorder–watch."

Her face fell. "That's it?" she asked.

"That's it for now," he said sweetly. "Even though it may not sound very exciting, it's *very* important that we have a record of who calls. It could lead us to the warheads."

"Okay," Theresa said, perking up a bit. "I won't let you down."

Uncle Sam cleared his throat. "Good. Jo, you're up."

Jo bounced up and down with excitement. "I thought you'd forgotten about me! Hang on a sec."

Uncle Sam laughed. "You're certainly in rare form tonight. Jo, you need to pay special attention to anyone the Nicholsons speak with from any foreign country since we suspect the group Jonathon is in cahoots with is definitely not a domestic one. Set up a file of people they talk to, countries they're from, matters discussed, that sort of thing."

"Gotcha," Jo said, smiling.

"That's it for now, ladies, unless you have anything else," Uncle Sam said.

"I have a mission for *you*," Jo replied mock huskily. "You have to let me know what you look like. It's a health precaution because I'm *dying* to know."

"Worry about the list, not my looks," he said, "and you'll be just fine."

"G reat, a *downpour*," Jo moaned as she walked out of the Ritz bright and early Thursday morning. "That's going to do wonders for my hair."

"Umbrellas up," Caylin said, clicking hers open.

As Theresa followed suit she spied a woman without an umbrella standing at the café across the street. "Check out that chick getting drenched over there!" she observed. "Wait—is that—?"

The short brown hair, the lean frame—where did Theresa know her from? Staring at her a moment longer, Theresa gasped as it clicked. It was *her*—the woman from the elevator. The shiny cap of hair was a dead giveaway. Without a word Theresa fished her lipstick camera out of her purse. She removed the cap, twisted up the red lipstick "lens," and hit the button on the bottom of the tube, which activated the shutter.

"Check it—it's her," Theresa whispered, clicking the lipstick cam as quickly as she could. "That creepy woman—over there." But by the time Jo and Caylin looked up, the mystery woman was nowhere in sight.

"You're probably imagining things, T.," Jo said.

"No!" Theresa looked at the empty space where Short Hair had been, her nerves frayed with frustration. "She was right there—the woman from the elevator, remember?"

"Oh yeah," Jo murmured. "I liked her hair."

"Well, now it's immortalized on film," Theresa said, holding up her lipstick cam. "I got some really great shots."

Caylin snatched the camera out of her hands. "Oh, I was so green when you got this! This is the glammest gadget going."

Jo stole it from Caylin. "How does it work?"

"Just point, click, and shoot," Theresa explained, saying cheese as Jo aimed it her way. "But seriously, this woman is following us."

"But seriously, you're being paranoid," Jo replied.

"I hope so," Theresa murmured. "For our safety's sake, I really do."

"I'm getting cramps already!" Caylin snickered as she crept toward the embassy bathroom. She scoped out the hall, shifty eyed, to make sure no one was around to blow her cover. But just as she was about to make a quick entrance a young executive type barreled out, high heels clickety-clacking on the tile floors.

"Good morning," Caylin said with a nod as she continued rolling her trash can down the hall, pail of cleaning supplies in hand. When the coast was clear, Caylin backtracked and ditched her supplies near the door so she could execute her operation unencumbered. Taking a deep breath, she ducked into the empty bathroom.

Operation On The Rag is now in full effect, Caylin thought as she placed five shillings into the machine and retrieved one tampon. It didn't feel all that special to her, so she dug out more shillings and cranked out more tampons to be safe.

What if someone walked off with my magic tampon? Caylin lamented, her stomach lurching with worry. Just then her five shillings were eaten up with a sickening clank—she'd bought every last tampon in the machine.

Suddenly the door swung open and an efficient-looking woman entered the bathroom. Caylin stifled a gasp, stuffed the tampons in her housedress pockets, and pretended to clean the machine with the sleeve of her dress.

"Good morning," the woman said. She eyed Caylin's pockets curiously.

"Can't hurt to be prepared, cannit?" Caylin replied, accent pitch perfect. Once the woman ducked in a stall, Caylin slipped into a stall of her own and began ripping open tampon after tampon. The fifth one revealed gold—eight bugs, just as Uncle Sam promised. She dumped the loot into the breast pocket of her housedress. Talk about my time of the month! she thought, chuckling softly.

No one answered when Caylin rapped on Jonathon's door—a very good sign.

"Housekeeping," she hollered, letting herself in. Her pulse quickened as she noticed a brown suitcase in front of the door. Jonathon was back in town! As excited as Caylin was to finally have the chance to see him in the flesh, right now she had other priorities.

"Mr. Nicholson?" she called, just in case he was asleep. No answer, no sign, no problem. But I've gotta move fast, she thought.

Surveillance search—check, Caylin noted as she scoped around for hidden cameras or any tape recorders. When her search came up empty, Caylin breathed a sigh of relief. At least no one had beaten her to the punch.

The first bug went under Jonathon's oak desk. The second, on the bedroom nightstand. The third, in the bathroom. Caylin installed them quickly and methodically, all that security training paying off in spades.

The last bug, destined for the phone, was a tad trickier. Caylin grabbed the receiver clumsily, twisting the top off the earpiece to place the bug inside. She replaced the earpiece, already cheering her success. But with a few turns of the earpiece left to go, it stuck. Just then the doorknob rattled.

Looks like I've got company, Caylin thought. She wrenched the earpiece on tightly, the intensity of the moment giving her extra speed. Without a second's panic she replaced the assembled phone on its cradle, grabbed her orange feather duster, and started dusting up a storm as the door opened with a bang.

"Just who are you, and *what* are you doing in my room?" Jonathon Nicholson demanded angrily.

Caylin jumped, totally taken aback by both Jonathon's tone and how hot his white-T-and-khakis-clad self was in person. The tousled brown hair! The sparkling dark eyes! The way his eyebrows scrunched up when he was mad! All the excuses she had planned to make went out of her head and up in smoke at the mere sight of him. But in order to save face, she made a split second decision to play off her moshing hormones as jitters.

"Cripes, settle down!" she shrieked. "I'm only the bloody housekeeper. Thanks a lot for scaring the living daylights out of me."

"Oh, uh, I'm sorry," Jonathon said, shutting the door with a guilty look on his face.

"You bloody well should be, giving an innocent girl the collywobbles like that."

Jonathon shrugged and approached the desk she was "dusting." "I'm really sorry. Honestly." He extended a Rolex-flanked hand. "Jonathon Nicholson."

"Louise Browning," she said, nearly falling over from the electric charge she felt as he grasped her hand in his.

"I'm William Nicholson's son," he explained, releasing his grip. "Interning for the summer."

"And scaring housekeepers to death while you're at it," Caylin joked flirtatiously.

He chuckled, meeting her starry-eyed gaze. "Yes, I guess I *am* doing that as well, Louise Browning."

She joined in the laughter. "Well, just don't let it happen again, Jonathon Nicholson."

He scratched his chin. "I just didn't expect anybody in here. The old housekeeper used to come at two o'clock every day. You could set your clock by her. Are you new?"

She nodded. "Yes, started yesterday and still trying to figure out this blasted cleaning schedule, I'm afraid. You weren't in yesterday, were you?"

"I was at a funeral in D.C.," Jonathon said, his features clouding slightly.

"I'm sorry to hear that. Family?"

"No. A friend."

Frank Devaroux, Caylin deduced. "I'll be out of your hair, then, so you can settle in."

He smiled again, his eyes crinkling at the corners. "Okay. Thanks."

For someone possibly involved in a murder, Caylin thought, he sure has looks that kill. As she gathered her things and bid adieu, however, Caylin reminded herself that she had to keep her mind off Jonathon's looks and on the mission at hand. But as she stole one last glance at him before walking out the door, she got the feeling that wasn't going to be easy at *all*.

*　　　*　　　*

Jo chowed down on a grilled cheese sandwich in the embassy commissary, lost in thought. Her morning had been utterly uneventful. The files Sandra wanted her to translate were endless, barely leaving her time to breathe, much less talk to any of the other translators. Plus Sandra kept bugging her about doing the music-for-the-ball thing, making Jo sincerely regret she'd ever offered to help in the first place. She desperately wanted to get the dirt on the Nicholsons. There'd been no chance thus far.

"Excuse me—is this seat taken?"

Jo jumped, startled, at the sound of the deep, sexy, Italian-inflected voice. Her heart raced and her breath grew shallow as she looked up from her sandwich into the black, black eyes of her fellow translator Antonio. While he smiled down at her over his lunch tray, she soaked in his olive skin and glossy, curly hair.

"Uh, um, yeah—I mean, no, it's not taken," she blurted, blushing slightly. Antonio wanted to sit with her! This was *definitely* enough to jump-start her afternoon.

"Thanks, Natascia," he said, sliding into the adjacent folding chair and tossing his silk paisley tie over his shoulder. "I couldn't ask for a prettier lunch partner."

Jo smiled. "Why, thanks. I bet you say that to all the girls."

"Only to translators with supermodel looks," he said, fixing her with an intense gaze before biting into his sandwich. Roast beef, double stuffed.

"Speaking of supermodels," Jo began, "what are you doing translating? With that face you could be on magazine covers from here to Timbuktu."

He smiled, mesmerizing her with his dimples. "Flattery will get you everywhere. But all that's holding me back from a glamorous life as a supermodel are my studies at Cambridge. International business."

All those looks—and brains, too! Jo marveled with a silent sigh. "Wow, a Cambridge man—I'm impressed. Do you like translating?"

"Pays the bills."

"Do you do a lot of translating for the Nicholsons?" she asked nonchalantly.

"Yes, some," he replied, taking a bite of his salad.

"Which languages?"

"Italian, Spanish, some Portuguese," he replied, an eyebrow raised. "Why do you ask?"

"Just curious. You know, I'm new to the job, so I'm interested in what goes on."

He looked deeply into her eyes. "Well, business is not my favorite subject, especially when I'm in the company of someone as beautiful as you."

Jo's face made like a candied apple. When she flirted with a scrumptious hottie, it usually didn't affect her like this—not at all. She'd heard lines like Antonio's before, millions of times. But the depth of his gaze gave her a completely unfamiliar sensation. He wasn't playing around, even though his words were. His eyes were compellingly serious.

"Well," she said, "hate to dine and dash, but I have an important errand, so if you'll excuse me . . ."

She grabbed her tray and bailed before she could fall even deeper under his spell.

Caylin dragged her gear back to the storage closet, groaning all the way. Even though she thrived on all-out physical exertion, exerting herself while *cleaning* was a million times more backbreaking. She'd never felt so sore in her life. Not even the memory of bugging William Nicholson's suite without a hitch could raise her enthusiasm.

"This job really sucks," she muttered, throwing her bucket in the corner angrily. It knocked over a bunch of mops that had been leaning precariously against the fuse box.

"Blast it!" Caylin wanted desperately to turn around and leave the mess behind. Of course, if she ended up getting fired, Uncle Sam would be none too pleased. Her next undercover assignment would be mowing the embassy lawn or something.

She picked up the mops and leaned them back up against the fuse box. The door of it was hanging slightly ajar, so she pushed it shut. The problem was, it wouldn't *stay* shut.

Impulsively Caylin opened the fuse box to find out what the problem was. She found a leather-bound date book nestled inside.

"What the . . . ?" She grabbed the date book and began leafing through it quickly. No distinguishing names, places, or phone numbers could be found—not immediately, anyway. She closed it and noticed that the smooth finish of the cover was marred by some sort of indented scribble. Like someone had used it as a table to support a piece of paper as they wrote.

Her curiosity in overdrive, Caylin held up the cover to the light and tried to make out what the scribble read. It was a series of numbers: 2025554357.

"Oh . . . my . . . gosh," she breathed. She recognized that number. Area code 202, 555-4357. The red line. Tower speak for the number to Uncle Sam's emergency phone.

"You're so lucky, Jo," Theresa griped in the middle of a crowded pub down the block from the Ritz. "*You* get to work with a cute guy. The closest I got today was taking a call from some weird guy named Albert or Alex or something. He kept calling me Gwenna instead of Emma."

"Maybe he got you confused with Gwyneth Paltrow, who *played* Emma," Jo suggested.

"I wish—at least then I'd have kissed Brad Pitt in my lifetime." Theresa sighed.

"Oh, come on, you get to talk to guys all day long," Jo teased. "You probably take a hundred calls a day from beautiful people of the male persuasion."

"Saying, 'Hello, U.S. Embassy,' isn't exactly what I'd call 'talking to guys,'" Theresa said with a laugh. "What kind of impact am I making on this investigation, anyway?"

"Logging all the calls that come in could be totally crucial to finding the list," Jo reasoned. "And if Caylin was able to bug the Nicholsons' suites, your log will help us figure out who the calls are from and when they came in."

"And if Caylin's phone bugs fail, I'll have backup," Theresa realized. "Hey, speaking of Caylin, where is she? She should have been here fifteen minutes ago."

"Not in trouble, I hope," Jo said, biting her lip. "Do you think—"

"There she is!" Theresa waved toward the door, where Caylin had just burst in, her hair mussed and her face flushed.

"Are you all right?" Jo asked, worried.

"I'm great," Caylin insisted as she took her seat. "You won't *believe* the day I had." She leaned her head confidentially toward the others. "Not only did I bug the suites," she whispered, "but . . . I think I found Frank Devaroux's date book."

"Oh, score!" Jo cheered softly.

Theresa clapped her hand to her mouth. "Where? How?"

Before Caylin could respond, a waitress appeared with a full tray of fish-and-chips. "*Bon appétit*," she said, setting the mighty meal on the table.

Caylin leaned back over the plate. "Listen, I'll give you the specs later," she murmured. "I had to run back to the hotel and stash that baby in the safe ASAP—that's why I'm late."

"Well, we've got the guy's handwriting samples in the safe, too, so I can run a check on that after dinner," Theresa suggested.

"Cool. I can't wait," Caylin said. "I'm so excited, I can hardly eat." She piled two pieces of fish and a handful of chips on her plate. "But I will, anyway," she added quickly.

"Okay, the conference is taking place two weeks from next Monday," Theresa began between bites. "It's the perfect place and time for Jonathon and his flunkies to announce they've got the lethal list—if they find it before we do, that is."

"Well, now that we've got a real lead, we could have this mission wrapped up by tomorrow," Jo pointed out.

"That'd be awesome," Caylin chimed in.

"Not exactly," Theresa said. "We shouldn't put all our hopes on this. We only have seventeen days until the conference, and we can't waste our time on false leads." She twirled a strand of hair around her index finger thoughtfully. "Seventeen days. It's not much time when you think about it."

Caylin gestured with a chip in her hand. "But if the world was made in seven days, we sure can solve this case in seventeen . . . can't we?"

*   *   *

"So Theresa compared the handwriting in the date book to the samples here in the safe, and it checks out," Caylin relayed to Uncle Sam via videophone. "It's Frank Devaroux's book, definitely."

"And get this," Theresa burst in. "At the top of last week's page he scrawled 'green disk' in big letters. So that probably means the list is stored on a disk somewhere. Was anything found on Devaroux when he was killed?"

"No," Uncle Sam replied. "If he had been carrying a disk, his killer or killers would have taken it. Obviously they don't have it and are still looking for it."

"How do you know?" Jo asked, arching an eyebrow.

"Well, I have big news for you, too, ladies. We picked up a phone conversation this afternoon between Jonathon Nicholson and someone known only as Alfred."

Theresa's eyes lit up. "Alfred! That's the guy I was talking about earlier—the one who sounded like a weirdo."

"Your instincts were definitely right," Uncle Sam said. "Take a listen."

There was a click, then some static. Then:

"Do you have the disk yet?"

"That's Alfred's voice," Theresa confirmed. "Totally."

"Negative."

"Jonathon Nicholson," Caylin identified. "No doubt."

"Any progress?" Alfred's recorded voice continued.

"I'm trying, but it's hard with everyone around."

"Well, time is ticking here."

"I know, I know," Jonathon replied, his recorded voice urgent. *"You'll get your disk, I assure you."*

"If I don't, you don't get the two million dollars wired into your account. You have until the conference."

There was a click, then silence.

After a few seconds Caylin exhaled shakily. "Man, that was—*whoa.*"

"What a slimeball to put the world's safety in jeopardy for a few lousy Benjamins," Jo spat out in disgust.

"Yeah, and for way less than Jim Carrey gets for one measly movie," Theresa joked halfheartedly.

Uncle Sam cleared his throat. "Well, Jim Carrey aside, that's all we've got so far."

"Between this call and the date book we know that the list is on a disk—and that's major," Theresa offered.

"And Devaroux probably stashed it somewhere in the embassy, just like he did with the date book," Caylin suggested.

"Speaking of which," Uncle Sam began, "you should courier that date book to me immediately."

"But what if there's more information in it?" Caylin complained.

"If you didn't find more tonight, there probably isn't any more. But I'll have my staff go over it with a fine-tooth comb and report back to you if they find anything. You don't have time to be analyzing that book. Anything else?"

"Tell you what," Theresa said. "If Alfred calls again, I won't put him through. That way maybe we can stall their operation."

"Good idea. Anything else?" Uncle Sam asked.

"Tell Uncle Sam about those pics you shot," Caylin urged Theresa.

"Oh yeah!" Theresa said, hitting her forehead with the palm of her hand. "I totally forgot—I took some pictures with my lipstick cam this morning. They're of this woman who appears to be trailing us. We've seen her two times now, and I have a bad feeling about her."

"Brown short hair?" he asked.

"Yes—how'd you know?" Theresa asked urgently.

"No reason," Uncle Sam said, voice smooth as silk. "Send the film along with the date book, and we'll investigate. But in the meantime concentrate first and foremost on finding that disk."

"But this woman could be the key to finding it," Theresa persisted.

"As I said, we'll investigate."

Theresa's brows knitted in confusion. Something very fishy was going on. Was Uncle Sam aware of Short Hair's identity and withholding information to protect them? Who cares, Theresa thought. All that matters are my instincts. And my instincts tell me this woman is really, really bad news.

6

"Mmmbop, ooh ohh mmmbop," Caylin sang off-key as she made her way to Jonathon's suite Friday morning. She'd been singing all morning, possibly because her whole outlook on cleaning had been changed after her discovery of Devaroux's date book. Today she found herself experiencing a sort of inner peace, as if she'd just had a good aromatherapy massage. But her chakras were quickly unaligned when she was practically knocked over by someone barreling out of the suite.

"Cor blimey!" she exclaimed as she looked up into the nearly unrecognizable face of Jonathon Nicholson. His once friendly smile had been replaced with a nasty scowl. "You almost knocked me over, there," she finished weakly.

"Well, you should watch where you're going," Jonathon growled, shooting her an icy glare.

"Looks like some bloke got up on the wrong side of the bed," Caylin said, her heart pounding anxiously. Deep inside, she was certain his mood had nothing to do with a bad night's sleep. The veins bulging at his temples and the white in the knuckles of his close-fisted hands told her only one thing: that he had found the bugs. Operation on the Rag was a bust, pure and simple.

"I don't have time to talk to the hired help," he said, his eyes slits.

"What's your bloody problem?" she asked, drop jawed.

"I don't have a problem. Just stay out of my way!" he warned, stomping down the hall.

"Don't worry—I wouldn't want to be within a hundred feet of your rude self," she muttered. But he was already gone.

She opened the door slowly, holding her ragged breath. With tightly crossed fingers she tiptoed into the bathroom. When she spotted the tiny black bug, she breathed a sigh of relief. She checked for the bugs one by one, only to find each firmly in place.

"What's Jonathon's deal?" she muttered. If he hadn't found out about the bugs, he must have found out *something*. But what?

I really need a mental health break, Jo thought. She leaned back from the desk and closed her eyes, ignoring the boring Portuguese document in front of her. She felt a light tap on her arm and jumped. She glanced up, ready to apologize to Sandra for loafing. Instead she stifled a gasp. The eyes she was looking into belonged to none other than Jonathon Nicholson!

"Yes?" she asked, trying to act clueless over his identity.

"I don't believe we've met." He extended a hand and flashed her a smile. "Jonathon Nicholson."

Jo struggled to keep the displeasure off her face. Slimeballs like Jonathon made her want to blow chunks. "Um, Natascia Sanchez," she said, shaking his hand and noticing its silky smoothness, the firm grip. Boy, do I have mixed feelings about this guy, she thought. Like someone took my emotions and tossed them in a Cuisinart or something.

"It's a pleasure," he replied, then looked around at the other translators. "Excuse me, everyone. I need to know if anyone here speaks Arabic."

"Um, a little," Jo lied, tentatively lifting her hand skyward. If Jonathon bought her baloney, she figured that could get her into a face-to-face meeting with the ringleader of this whole she-bang. She could always get The Tower to wire her to a real Arabic translator or something so no one would ever be the wiser. She certainly couldn't do that this very second, however. "I'm . . . I'm pretty rusty, though, and I'm also *totally* busy with this document—"

"Yes, I can see that," Jonathon said, a look of genuine relief flooding his handsome features. "Well, I don't need your services just yet, but I'll definitely be in touch."

As he departed, Jo bit her lip. She was happy her boss wasn't in to witness her white lie, but she *really* hoped she wasn't in over her head.

*   *   *

"TGIF," Caylin said, kicking off her shoes the moment she entered the hotel suite. "Ugh! Thank goodness I've got Monday off. I don't think I can take much more of this."

"Yeah, we've got Monday off, too," Theresa said with a wave, her eyes glued to the TV set. "What's this bank holiday thing all about, anyway?"

"It's kinda like Presidents' Day, but it happens three times a year," Jo explained. "Sandra told us non–Brit translators all about it." She sighed. "Listen, change of subject. I told a huge lie today, and I'm really worried I messed up."

"What about?" Caylin asked, pausing in the doorway.

"She told Jonathon she spoke Arabic," Theresa said. "I told her it was no biggie."

"Well, he *asked,* and I said I did just in case it had something to do with the disk," Jo admitted, stomach clenching.

"You were *improvising,* not screwing up," Caylin told her. "Give me a break. You had the chance of a lifetime and you took it. I'd have done the same thing."

"Yeah, I guess it's not so bad," Jo lied. She smiled confidently, but inside she was all butterflies. "But now I hope I *don't* get to make good on it. If I have to get wired to a translator, I'll scream. Those stupid things are so itchy, and I'd have to wear a baggy blazer to hide it." She shivered. "If it ain't tight, it ain't right—that's my motto."

Theresa laughed. "Hey, hurry up and get

changed, Cay. I got an E-mail from Uncle Sam, and we're supposed to check in tonight. Something about a new assignment."

"Well, do *I* have a story for him," Caylin called, voice slightly muffled. "And maybe he has a story or two for us about Devaroux's date book. I'll be out in two shakes."

As soon as she returned to the living room in a sweatshirt and jeans Caylin dialed Uncle Sam. Jo's anxiety mounted with each digit she punched.

"Hello, ladies," Uncle Sam said, a Will Smith poster hanging in place of his silhouette.

Jo laughed in spite of herself. "Whoa, Sam, cuttin' loose!"

"I always suspected you were a Man in Black," Theresa joked.

"Okay, okay—so he's gettin' jiggy wit' it," Caylin said impatiently. "Listen, something weird happened today."

"What is it?" Uncle Sam asked.

"Jonathon was completely rude to me," she said. "This, after he was so sweet to me yesterday. The bugs are all copacetic, but still, I think he may be on to me or something."

"Don't jump to conclusions," Uncle Sam suggested. "Anyone else have any contact with him today?"

Jo nodded, taking a deep breath. "Well, he came in and introduced himself, then asked us—the translators—if we spoke Arabic. Then I, uh, told him I did, even though I don't. I just didn't know what else to do." She paused, feeling sick to her stomach. "I mean—I don't speak Arabic, obviously, but what if this is the key that we need?"

"Don't worry," he said after a beat, instantly alleviating Jo's tension. "You did the right thing. We could easily cover you when the time comes. But he wasn't rude or upset when he came into the translation office?"

"Quite the contrary, really," Jo said in relief. "All smiles."

"Well, how about you, Theresa?" Uncle Sam asked. "Anything?"

She shook her head. "Not a thing. I guess Friday is a slow day on the phones. I have absolutely nothing to report. Not even a call from Alfred."

"That's okay," Uncle Sam said. "You'll have lots to do next week after the holiday. Caylin, I'd like you to plant some bugs in the Nicholsons' offices on Tuesday—those will be ready at the hotel desk Monday afternoon in a faux tube of toothpaste."

"Check," Caylin croaked out. She sounded almost bored by the idea. "Hey, was there any word on Devaroux's date book?"

"Clean as a whistle," Uncle Sam replied. "Nothing that appears to be of any importance."

Caylin swore under her breath. From the looks of her, it was hard to tell if she was inspecting her split ends or about to tear her hair out. Theresa slumped back against the couch, deflated. She picked up a Ritz notepad and began scribbling on it aimlessly. The sight of them made Jo's heart sink along with her spirits. Getting nowhere was getting the best of them all.

"May I make a suggestion?" Jo asked, breaking the silence. "Considering Caylin's run-in with Jonathon and my little stress attack, maybe we should take it easy this weekend. See the sights, have some fun. We've been kind of missing out in those departments lately, and I think we could use a break."

"There's not much we can do in the embassy on a weekend, anyway," Theresa added.

"I have to agree," Caylin chimed in. "I'm feeling a little frustrated, to be honest. It's really ticking me off."

"Well, unless an emergency development arises, consider yourselves on vacation till Tuesday," Uncle Sam announced.

Jo cheered. The news was music to her ears. She *needed* a break, that was for sure. She looked at the others in glee. Caylin had perked up instantly, and Theresa was drawing a big smiley face on the memo pad. They were ready for London, all righty. She just hoped London was ready for them.

After a full Saturday of shopping till they dropped, Jo, Caylin, and Theresa rode the elevator up to the fourteenth floor of the Ritz, arms overloaded with packages and their weekly Tower stipends almost exhausted.

"I can't believe you bought three stuffed animals and no clothes, T.," Jo said in confusion.

"I love animals way more than I love outfits," Theresa said, not one bit embarrassed. "These were too cute to resist."

"To each his own." Caylin laughed. "I'm just happy I got all this yummy bath stuff. This is really going to relax me."

As they entered the suite Jo said, "Right now we need to do the *opposite* of relaxing. What do you say to a night on the town? We can get dolled up and head out to the nearest club. I hear they get pretty crazy here—all ages, techno music, nonalcoholic smart drinks, dancing till dawn. How 'bout it?"

Caylin jumped up and down with excitement. "Sounds awesome, possum!"

"I don't know . . . ," Theresa said nervously. "We don't really know our way around yet."

"So we'll take a cab," Jo said, running to her closet. "It's time to let loose, Theresa."

Without a word Theresa went into the nearest bathroom and stared into the mirror. Looking back was a cute girl in the prime of her life who was too scared to live it. Well, she wasn't holding herself back anymore.

"Does anybody have a bright red lipstick I could borrow?" Theresa called, running a finger over her naked lips. "My lipstick cam isn't going to cut it tonight!"

Meltdown, "the hottest club in the galaxy," according to the cabdriver, was crammed to the gills.

Caylin immediately dashed onto the dance floor and began tearing it up in her little red dress and stiletto heels. She didn't care that she didn't have a partner—she was sure there wasn't a guy in town who could keep up with her, anyway. For Caylin, dancing was a totally personal issue, one that didn't need to be shared. She closed her eyes, letting the ambient beats carry her far away from her stress and into the zone where nothing mattered but music and movement.

She immersed herself in full bliss, but a light body slam jarred her out of it abruptly. She whirled around and saw Theresa giggling madly in her black jeans and baby T.

"You go, girl!" Theresa hollered over the music. "How can you dance to this stuff? It's so . . . bland."

"Techno rules!" Caylin shimmied to the quickening beat. "Come on, you try it."

"No way," Theresa demurred. "I can't dance when the music's got no soul."

"I can't believe you're not into this stuff, *techie.*"

"Hey, computers are good for a lot of things, but making music is *not* one of them." Theresa bounced up and down to the beat. "I feel so stupid!"

"Who cares? Have some fun for once." Caylin spun around and spotted Jo at the edge of the dance floor, looking beyond stunning in her white Armani halter dress. She was flirting madly with two guys at the same time. When another guy rushed over to give her a drink, Caylin burst out laughing.

She glanced away toward the bar, where someone appeared to be giving her the eye. A woman, she realized. She froze instantly. The brunette sat alone, sipping a glass of something orange. She looked familiar—a little *too* familiar.

The realization hit Caylin like a bolt of lightning: Short Hair! Her pulse raced out of control as she watched the woman take a dainty sip of her drink, suddenly oblivious to Caylin's stare down.

"What's wrong?" Theresa asked over the music. "Is this a bad song? I can't tell the diff—"

"Short Hair! At the bar!"

Alarm clouded Theresa's features. "What? Where?"

Caylin pointed back over her shoulder. She scanned the crowd for Jo but couldn't find her anywhere. A tap on her shoulder sent her reeling around, ready to drop-kick Short Hair in a millisecond.

"Hey! Hey!" Jo yelled, holding her hands up defensively. "Some freaky moves you've got there, *Jackie Chan!*"

"Okay, here comes the strategy," Caylin announced in the middle of the dance floor. "We chase Short Hair down and demand to know why she's following us. Tell her we have photographic evidence. Theresa's been right all along—this woman's obviously working for the enemy. Let's rock!"

Caylin darted off instantly before Jo could

even begin to process the information. Shrugging, Jo followed, weaving and pushing her way through the thick crowd, making about an inch per hour. Her left ankle buckled as her platform sandal skidded on the drink-slick floor. With a sigh of lament she kicked off her sandals completely. She'd be better off with grungy feet than a sprain, after all. Barefoot, Jo struggled to catch up, grimacing as she ran over pools of sticky spilt drinks and gross cigarette butts. Suddenly the music cut off and the club went totally dark. Jo stopped in place, blinded.

"Uh, we're the Scorching Radiators," a guy announced over the PA.

Jo turned around and saw a spotlit Trent Reznor look-alike front and center on the stage. He made chopping motions at a silver guitar. "Check—one, two. *Onetwothreefour!*"

Painfully loud industrial noise filled the club as the lights went back up. A mosh pit quickly formed, clogging Jo's path to the bar. She ground her teeth in frustration as she was battered back and forth. Her bare feet were definitely in danger, but it hardly mattered. She had to find Caylin and grab Short Hair before she got away.

With a shock Jo looked up to see someone being passed over her head—someone in a tiny red dress who was kicking angrily at the moshers with stiletto heels. Caylin! In a second she was whisked away, out of Jo's reach. Undaunted, Jo pushed ahead, desperate to make it to the bar. But when she was about midway through the pit, Short Hair's gaze met hers and she instantly ducked into the thickening wave of people. Cursing, Jo turned sharply left and bulleted forward. She immediately ricocheted off a burly guy in a satin rugby shirt.

"Watch it!" he bellowed. His drink toppled and spilled all over her white dress. Probably on purpose. She hardly noticed as she squeezed past him and searched frantically for the black leather outfit, the tall frame, the pouty lips. But all of the above were MIA at the moment.

"Wait—there she is—over there!" Theresa screamed over the noise. She ran like mad after the glossy cap of brown hair and spotted a barefoot, drink-stained apparition on her right. "Don't just stand there!" she hollered, grabbing Jo by the arm and yanking her in the right direction.

"Excuse me! Excuse me!" Theresa barreled into people left and right. Thank goodness I put aside my computer long enough to go to all those Fugazi shows, she thought proudly as she slammed her way through the crowd like a pro linebacker. A supermodel-looking girlie practically bounced off her shoulder.

"What in blazes are you doing?" she screeched.

"Emergency situation," Theresa yelled, pointing back to Jo. "This girl needs medical attention!"

Jo nodded. "Appendicitis. Don't drink the cranberry juice."

"Uh, okay," the girl said, stepping aside. Others around her followed suit, clearing a path for them.

"I see her—that way!" Theresa called, pointing to the front door. She hauled tail with all her might. Short Hair was barely two yards away. Suddenly an immense shadow grew along the floor, followed by an enormous wave of excited chatter. Before Theresa could stop and change direction, a huge group of under-eighteens rushed in past the bouncer.

"Stop!" Theresa screamed. She knew the momentum she had built up was about to work against her in a dangerous way, but she was powerless to prevent it. She careened headfirst into the crowd and was bounced clear off her feet and onto the floor. A very sturdy Dr. Marten boot kicked her to add insult to injury. By the time she clambered to her feet, Short Hair was gone.

Infuriated, Theresa threw herself back down on the floor. "I think I'll just stay down here a while, if you don't mind," she told Jo's sorry-looking feet.

A hand dangled in front of her face. Theresa looked up to see Caylin, scowling. Her blond hair was in an insane tangle, and her right stiletto heel was missing and presumed dead somewhere in the pit. She pulled Theresa to her feet with a slight stumble. Cursing, she lifted up her left foot and snapped off the heel of her shoe as if it were a twig. "This is pointless!" she hollered, throwing the heel to the ground.

"Well . . . at least we know she's on to us," Jo said optimistically.

"A whole lot of good that does us now," Theresa muttered. If they couldn't beat the mosh pit at Meltdown, how were they supposed to stop a gang of ruthless terrorists from destroying the world?

7

H ello?" Caylin said briskly into the phone Monday afternoon, feeling refreshed and revived after a Sunday of doing nothing but sleeping and recharging. But since Jo and Theresa had called dibs on a holiday stroll, Caylin was forced to stay in and play secretary in case Uncle Sam called in with an emergency.

"Yes, Louise Browning, please," said a woman who sounded an awful lot like her boss, Fiona.

Caylin gulped, wondering what her next move should be. She had answered the phone in her normal voice, so she couldn't just say, "Speaking."

"One moment, please," she said, adding a little bit of country twang to her own Maine accent. She rustled the phone a bit and waited about fifteen seconds for authenticity's sake.

"'Allo," she greeted Fiona in her Louise voice, adding a breathless element as if she had just rushed to the phone.

"Fiona here," she chirped. "Hate to ring you on holiday, but the weekend girl's come down with a bug. Could you possibly cover for her tonight? You'll get overtime pay."

"Why, sure," Caylin replied, trying to disguise her excitement. What better time to plant the bugs and search for the disk than when the offices were empty? "I could be there as soon as you need me, actually."

"Brilliant," Fiona said, very pleased. "Just be there around seven. I won't be there, but a schedule of offices you'll need to clean will be with the security copper. Simply ask for it when you sign in."

"Splendid," Caylin said, not quite believing her good fortune.

At twenty to seven Caylin swung by the front desk, her backpack stuffed to bursting, to pick up her "toothpaste." After she'd secured it, she ducked into the Ritz's ladies' lounge and cut the tube open with her Swiss army knife. There they were, eight more bugs. She hid them in her hair with bobby pins. This way, in the event that the security guard decided to frisk her or put her bags through the X ray, her bugs would pass for funky barrettes rather than ultrasophisticated surveillance equipment.

Caylin practically skipped all the way to the embassy. Not only was she psyched to come in on a holiday, but she'd be solo all evening, too. No Jonathon Nicholson to gripe her out, no Fiona inspecting her every move, no annoying crowds clogging the narrow halls. Bugging the Nicholsons' offices would be a megacinch!

"Nice barrettes," the security guard commented as she buzzed Caylin in.

"Thanks," Caylin replied. "I made them myself."

Without passing go or collecting two hundred dollars, Caylin headed straight to Jonathon's office. But just as she was about to bug the telephone, she heard approaching footsteps. Her heartbeat racing, she ducked under the desk and tried not to breathe too loudly.

"Hello, Louise?" a female voice—Fiona's!—screeched loudly. "Louise?"

What is Fiona doing here? Caylin wondered. She said she wasn't going to be in! Caylin bit her lip and scowled. This certainly would throw a wrench into the works.

When Fiona's footsteps finally faded into the distance, Caylin hopped up and finished the phone job hurriedly, totally on edge. She wasn't sure if Fiona would be back or what, but she wasn't taking any chances.

After she placed a bug in Jonathon's desk drawer, Caylin tackled the huge sliding glass door that led out to the balcony. But just as she was about to apply a bug in the lower corner, she heard footsteps approaching once more. Darn, she thought, Fiona again! The desk was on the other side of the office—her only way out was right in front of her. She was balcony bound.

Caylin gathered up her backpack, flipped up the security lock on the door, and slid it open quickly; thank goodness it was whisper quiet. In a flash she stepped out onto the narrow balcony and whisked the door shut.

What a horrid view! she thought, looking down the six floors onto an empty warehouse and an alley. She listened for some kind of sound on the other side of the glass door, but she heard nothing. She didn't see any shadows on the wall, either. The longer she waited, the more impatient she became. Surely Fiona would have come and gone by now.

She peeked through the door and gasped. There, in front of the desk, stood someone who was decidedly taller, more solidly built, and far more masculine than Fiona. It's Jonathon! Caylin realized, her spine tingling. And—oh no!—he was coming her way!

Caylin pulled her head back from the door and froze for a moment. She had absolutely nowhere to hide. Her heart beat a mile a minute. Terrified, she scooted as far away from the window as she could and plastered herself up against the embassy wall. Still no sign of Jonathon at the glass door. She was safe.

Suddenly a face pressed up against the door. Jonathon! Caylin bit her tongue to keep from screaming. Her heart beat so loudly, she was sure it would give her away. She tried not to move an inch, to breathe—she even tried to use her meditation techniques to become one with the wall. But her mind kept telling her she was dead meat. She shut her eyes and waited for the inevitable—for him to come out and throw her off the balcony.

She waited for what seemed like hours. Summoning all her courage, she opened her eyes. Jonathon's face was gone. And finally, after what seemed like an eternity, she heard the door inside open, close, and lock.

"I made it," Caylin murmured under her breath. "I'm alive. I made it." She peeked through the glass door—the office truly was empty. But when Caylin tried to open the door, it wouldn't budge. Jonathon had locked it.

"Just my luck," she muttered. What on earth was Jonathon doing in his office on a holiday, anyway? Didn't he have a *life*?

"Stay calm," Caylin told herself, taking a long, deep breath. She exhaled and began methodically removing her rappelling gear from her backpack. Thankfully she was only six floors up. Scaling down the embassy would be a walk in Hyde Park compared to the death-defying descents she'd made with her dad on some of their father-daughter mountaineering journeys. That didn't mean it was going to be easy, however.

After slipping off her gray housecoat to reveal a black bodysuit and tights, she quickly changed into her lightweight footwear and tied the housecoat around her waist. The service key! she remembered with a start. It was useless on the glass door, but she sure needed it to get back into Jonathon's office. She detached it from the key chain and hooked it onto her hoop earring for safekeeping.

Caylin strapped on her harness, hooked it up

to the line, and secured the other end of the line to the balcony rail. She tugged on it to make sure the connection was solid. After she wiped the sweat from her palms, she grabbed on to the end of the line nearest the balcony. On a wing and a prayer she boosted herself up onto the rail, swung her legs over, and dropped down over the side.

Her heart pounded fiercely—half from excitement, half from fear—as she swung freely under the balcony. The rush was intense. Her nerve endings were practically singing. With a grunt she swung her legs up so her feet met the wall. Pulling the line taut, she began walking down the side of the embassy, letting out a little line with each step.

Fifth floor . . . fourth floor . . .

As she descended she felt eerily calm—the way she always felt while doing something intensely physical. But this time the stakes were different. Her backpack was splayed out where her "boss" could find it, totally blow her cover, and bring her career as a spy to a screaming halt. Her line was hooked to the balcony of a terrorist who could rush out and send her plummeting to her death without a second thought.

Caylin's palms immediately went into a sweat. She lost her grip momentarily and slipped down the rope. In her free fall the air whooshed out of her lungs. She couldn't breathe. She couldn't scream.

With a thud she landed on the third-floor balcony.

"Third floor," she murmured. "Housewares, lingerie, and *time to get a grip, Caylin.*" Thankfully the room on the other side of the glass door was abandoned. She'd hate to have all that awful explaining to do while her butt was aching.

Glowering, she wiped her palms on the housecoat and pitched herself over the balcony for the last half of the ride. She rushed herself—not a smart move where safety was concerned, but she had no time to waste. Her nerves were jangling anxiously, and she lost her foothold a couple of times. But she wanted to get her toes on solid ground and her tail back up to Jonathon's office before Jonathon—or Fiona, even—could catch a drift of her little ruse.

She slid all the way down the line from the second-floor balcony, silently cheering as she touched down. With lightning speed she disconnected herself from the rope, brushed off, and slipped into her uniform. She left her harness connected to the rope—she'd pull it up once she made it back to Jonathon's office.

If I get there in time, that is, she thought with a wince. Sheer panic flooded her body. Mortified, she unsuccessfully smoothed out the wrinkles in her housecoat and prayed no one would ask her where she got such weird-looking shoes.

Caylin knew her confidence wasn't about to return anytime soon, but she didn't have time to wait for it. She rushed toward the rear security entrance. She didn't want the woman up front wondering where she'd lost her fabulous barrettes.

"I can't bloody believe this, but I was taking out the trash and got locked out," Caylin ranted before the rear security guard could open his mouth. "Cripes, I'm not even supposed to work today and I get stuck out in the wind! Can't believe my luck. I really bloody can't."

The overweight security guard, engrossed in his *Sun* tabloid, barely even looked up during her entire monologue. Finally his gaze met hers. "No bother," he muttered, buzzing her in.

Once in, Caylin raced to the elevator and back up to Jonathon's office without encountering another soul. She removed the key from her earring and opened the door. The office looked exactly how she'd left it. And the balcony—*yes!* Her hook glimmered through the glass door. She put on her rubber cleaning gloves, undid the lock, and stepped out onto the balcony, wanting to drop to her knees and kiss her untouched backpack and even her ugly embassy-issue housekeeping shoes.

"What in the world are you doing out there?"

"F-Fiona!" Caylin whirled around and gave her boss what she hoped was a confident smile. "Well, Jonathon asked me to dust off the balcony of his suite the other day," she lied, heart pounding like crazy as she positioned her body in front of the hook. "I figured I'd do it for his office as well."

Fiona eyed her suspiciously, but Caylin's

innocent gaze didn't waver one bit. "Oh, well, all right, then," Fiona said. "I was just wondering where you'd run off to. Security called me down to confirm you were the right girl and all. Everyone's high-strung round here with the conference just two weeks away, and I just wanted to suss everything out."

Caylin exhaled in relief. "Everything's right as rain, Fiona. I'm working like a busy bee. In fact, I'd climb the walls if you gave the word."

8

I've got the munchies in a *big* way," Theresa declared. Even though she'd only made it a couple of hours past lunch—shepherd's pie, the Tuesday special at the embassy commissary—she was feeling the need for something cocoa derived to combat the starch in her stomach. Desperate, she turned to the young woman at the voice mail station to her right for advice. "Siobhan, do you know if there are any vending machines in this place?" she asked breathlessly.

Siobhan looked at her questioningly. "You mean, candy machines and the like?"

"Yes!"

"Sorry, no," Siobhan replied. "But you might try the kitchen. I've snuck in there a few times m'self when I'm feeling peckish."

"Great. Do you want anything?"

"Ta, but no. Go on—I'll cover for you."

"Thanks, Siobhan." In a flash Theresa was out of her seat and motoring down the hall, visions of chocolate cake, chocolate pudding, and chocolate chocolate dancing before her eyes. As she made her way down the hall she kept extra vigilant. She hoped no one would see her sneak in and get suspicious. As a guy passed her in the otherwise empty hallway she nodded uncomfortably. Her palms were sweaty, trembling. She needed a chocolate fix *bad*.

She burst through the kitchen doors and made a beeline for the fridge. But as she sifted through it her spirits sank. There was nothing rich and sinfully delicious in sight. There wasn't even anything brown. She *did* find, to her amazement, some bottles of nail polish, a few prescription drug vials, and even a crystal vase. *Not* the kinds of things regularly served at the commissary. She felt as if she'd stumbled on someone's stash of goodies.

Ding! went the brilliance bell in Theresa's head. A kitchen is an awfully good place to hide something that isn't food related, she realized. Maybe I should have a look around while I have the place to myself. If Caylin found a date book in a fuse box, why couldn't she find a top secret disk in the kitchen?

She started with the cabinets, pulling everything out and feeling along the bottom of large cans and bowls for anything suspicious. She even felt along the shelf paper but to no avail. Next came the drawers. Still no luck.

Once she had removed nearly all the refrigerator's contents onto the kitchen floor for inspection, she panicked. She *definitely* heard the commissary door open. Oh no, she thought, terrified. Who could it be—and how exactly was she supposed to explain away the mess? She hoped it was just someone cleaning the commissary tables, but she couldn't rely on hope anymore. In a total frenzy she scrambled to cram everything back into the fridge. A carton of eggs opened in the mayhem, and one crashed to the floor.

"Oh, *pretzels*," she mumbled. As she searched for a paper towel she heard someone clear his throat loudly. She held her breath and looked to her left. Immaculate brown hair, a tall, toned frame, golden skin—Jonathon Nicholson!

"Who the heck are you?" Jonathon demanded, his tone nasty.

She lowered her gaze, feeling like a reprimanded schoolgirl. "Emma Webster," she answered. "Voice mail technician."

"What are you looking for?" he asked suspiciously.

"My, uh—," she stammered.

"Yes?" he demanded.

Her heart hammered, and her eyes began to water. "My, uh, asthma medication," she muttered, remembering the asthma inhaler cam in her purse. "I brought it to work, and Ms. Dalton said she'd stick it in the kitchen for me, but now I can't find it anywhere." She weakly picked up the prescription vials she'd found to support her fib. "And I—am— having—a—hard—time—breathing."

Theresa began to fake an asthma attack, gasping for breath as hard and convincingly as she could.

Her best friend back home had asthma, so she had witnessed a few attacks.

Jonathon's eyes grew wide. "Oh, my gosh, sit down. Do you need a paper bag to breathe into or something?"

She motioned to her purse, which he brought over to her double quick. She quickly retrieved her inhaler cam from the bottom of it, put it in her mouth, and pushed down. Instead of releasing medicine like a real inhaler, it snapped a pic of Jonathon. Up close, his eyes looked puffy—so much so, she was tempted to ask him about it.

Once she got the snaps she needed, her "asthma attack" miraculously ended. "Whoa, looks like I'm getting my air back," Theresa said, breathing an exaggerated sigh of relief. "Thank you so much for your help."

"No problem."

Theresa waved, deciding to leave the refrigerator items on the floor, egg and all, for extra effect. "Well, bye."

"Bye," Jonathon said, giving her a questioning look as she departed.

Did I make him suspicious? she wondered anxiously as she tried to mentally process his look. No, maybe . . . maybe he's just worried about me! The idea made her swoon—half in enchantment, half in amusement. Imagine a cold-blooded killer getting all weak hearted over a girl with asthma!

*   *   *

"So he looked all upset, and his eyes were red," Theresa relayed that night in 1423.

"I might know why," Caylin said, waving a fax. "This just came in from The Tower. Alfred called again at fifteen hundred hours and told Jonathon if he didn't get his disk by the conference, his father was going to be killed. Transcript right here."

"Oh, my gosh, no wonder!" Theresa exclaimed. "I'm such a jerk. That's when I was in the kitchen. Siobhan was covering for me, and she must have patched his call through!"

"Don't worry about it," Jo said. "It's a good thing you did—otherwise we wouldn't have found out this info."

"You know, you kind of have to feel sorry for the guy," Caylin commented. "He's totally in over his head."

Jo snorted. "He's a total scumbag. He puts his own father's life on the line for a pile of dough."

Theresa shrugged, not sure what to think. His swollen eyes had definitely looked as if they'd shed some major tears, so maybe he was genuinely upset. But if he was so upset about it, why was he going through with it?

"Well, no matter what we do or don't think about Jonathon," Caylin began, "the pressure's on to find this disk. At least Theresa was making an effort to find it today, unlike the rest of us. We've gotta move, and we've gotta move now."

"The key word is *green*," Theresa reminded them. "Is there anyplace in the embassy related to

101

the color green? The kitchen's out, but maybe some of the rooms have green walls."

"Maybe it's hidden in a green book in the library," Jo said.

"Or a greenhouse, if there is one," Caylin suggested.

Theresa chewed her nails. "Too many possibilities. My brain's going to crash just thinking about them."

"Well, we've got to get on this double quick," Caylin said. "We lost our steam after that night at Meltdown, but we need to get it back. I, for one, have a surprise in my backpack—Jonathon's trash. I snagged it today when I was cleaning."

"Oh, joy," Jo muttered. All this talk about William Nicholson's possible fate gave her an ugly feeling of déjà vu, and the thought of digging through his loser son's trash did nothing to improve her mood.

"Hopefully there's nothing too gross in here," Caylin said, crossing her fingers as she laid out some newspaper on the coffee table and placed the bag on top. "Jo, would you do the honors since you have the longest nails?"

"Whatever," Jo griped, slicing the bag with a long red nail.

Caylin dumped out the contents. A receipt from a corner deli, a half-empty bag of salt-and-vinegar potato chips, a banana peel, a coffee cup, some crumbled-up junk mail, and some miscellaneous scraps of paper. Nothing terribly exciting.

"Any of this look useful to you guys?" Theresa asked.

Jo sifted through the lot with disdain. "Hardly."

"Hey—look at this business card," Caylin said, snatching it up. "It's a nearby hotel. Maybe he stayed there so he could have some privacy."

"So he could make private phone calls, perhaps," Theresa suggested. "You know, so his father wouldn't overhear him?"

"There's only one way to find out," Caylin announced. "Pass me the phone, *por favor.*"

"Five Sumner Place—may I help you?"

"Yes, you may," Caylin began, putting a stuffy spin on her working-class Louise accent. "This is Veronica Carey, Jonathon Nicholson's secretary, and I believe he recently stayed there. If it's not too much trouble, I just need to confirm the day and time he checked out for his expense report."

"Very well, Ms.—Carey, was it?" the clerk said.

Caylin smiled confidently. "Yes. C-a-r-e-y. And while you've got the file handy, could you check and see if he made any calls? He never writes any of this stuff in, it's a bloody mess, and I'm left to sort through the fallout."

The clerk laughed. "My boss is like that, too."

Caylin heard the sound of computer keys clicking and crossed her fingers.

"Let's see," the clerk said, "he checked in yesterday at nine P.M. and out this morning at seven forty-five A.M. And there were four calls, all to the same international number."

"What country?" Caylin asked, hoping she wasn't pushing her luck. "I have to file them under different codes, you know."

"Hold on just a moment, please," the clerk said. "I'm looking that up for you."

Caylin held her breath.

"Ms. Carey?" the clerk asked. "That international country code indicates the call was placed to Laqui Bay."

Caylin stifled a gasp. "Ta," she said in shock before she hung up the phone.

"Any luck?" Jo asked halfheartedly.

"You're not going to like this one bit," Caylin began, her heart pounding. "But the call was made to Laqui Bay."

"*What?*" Jo shrieked, her eyes wide with disbelief.

"No way." Theresa shook her head. "This is incredible! You mean *the* Laqui Bay?"

"Like there's another one?" Caylin quipped with a snort. "Listen, if there was a different island called Laqui Bay, they should be searching for a new name double quick."

"Seriously," Theresa breathed. "I mean, it'd reek to be mistaken for the place responsible for bombing that jet last year—"

"Or for taking all those hostages in that awful subway incident—remember?" Jo added.

"*Or* for threatening world security by claiming

possession of nuclear missiles," Caylin suggested with a serious nod.

"That's right!" Theresa snapped her fingers. "Hey, maybe that threat was just wishful thinking. Maybe it was jumping the gun—"

"Until they got their hands on the warheads list," Caylin finished. "Well, if they think it's that easy, they've got another thing coming."

"I don't know," Theresa said, glowering. "If we think we can take on Laqui Bay, I'd say *we've* got another thing coming."

Get out of my office and *never* come back!"

"What?" Caylin screeched, terror coursing through her veins as the brick solid figure of Jonathon Nicholson confronted her after one single baby step into his office.

"You heard me—out. From now on I'm doing my own cleaning." He stormed over to the door and held it open. His dark eyes shot sparks at her, virtually daring her to protest.

"What's your bloody problem?" she asked, hoping to get at least one tiny morsel of information out of him. If he was busting her, anyway, what would it hurt to push?

"It's none of your *bloody* business," he hollered with a sarcastic, mimicking tone. "Now get out and stay out."

As Caylin followed his orders her head spun with worry. If he had finally realized she was the babe with the bugs, he could blow the mission—and possibly the entire world—sky-high. Either that or he'd just knock her off himself. Either way she was one dead dame.

At lunch Caylin ran to the Ritz to see if Uncle

Sam had been in contact. The following message was in the laptop's incoming mailbox:

> *J.N. office transmitters discovered this morning 8 A.M. followed by suite 8:15. Static received on all stations. Lay low until video conference tonight.*
>
> —*Uncle S.*

So Jonathon *was* buggin' over the bugs, Caylin thought with a sinking heart as she headed back to the embassy. She skulked into the utility room and jumped about a mile in shock. Fiona sat in wait for her, an evil look on her face. "Do you know anything about these silly devices found in the Nicholsons' offices and suites?" she demanded.

"What . . . devices?" Caylin asked innocently.

"The ones found in the Nicholsons' offices and suites," Fiona repeated slowly, as if she were speaking to a kindergartner. "Surveillance stuff. Spy gear. *Bugs*, I think they're called?"

"I have no clue what you're talking about," Caylin said with an edge of offense. "You know, Jonathon went off on me this morning, and I was wondering what his blimey problem was."

"That's it," Fiona said, cracking a smile. "I got the riot act myself, so don't feel bad. The suites are now off-limits to the cleaning staff, as are the Nicholsons' offices. Less bally work for us, right? And I hear they think some translator did it, anyway, so there's really no need to worry. But I had to ask."

Caylin nodded understandingly, trying her hardest not to look upset. A translator? she asked herself. That could only be one person . . . Jo!

Jo sipped her carrot juice and drank in the afternoon sunshine, a precious rarity. Pentland's, an outdoor café near the hotel, was the perfect place for a lunchtime getaway. The commissary's Wednesday meal du jour, bangers and mash, was hardly anything to write home about, and she really needed the private time. She wasn't used to being around people 24/7, being an only child and all. When her aunt and uncle had adopted her, they had given her the space and solitude she had grown accustomed to. Two things she hadn't had much of since coming to London, that was for sure.

"May I join you?" a familiar voice asked, breaking into her thoughts. Her skin tingled as she looked up from her journal to see Antonio, a charming smile playing on his lips.

"Okay," she said, figuring she could easily sacrifice her private moment for a flirt sesh. As long as she didn't let it get *too* intense. "How's it going?"

"Pretty good," he replied, taking a sip from his steaming cappuccino. "Work's been a killer, right?"

"That's for sure," she agreed, though work was the *least* of her problems.

"I'd give anything to jump in my Porsche right

now and take a few spins around a racetrack," he said with a sigh.

"You race?" she asked in amazement.

"Oh yeah, I love it," he said. "You too?"

"That's an understatement. I *live* for it!" She leaned back in her chair and twirled the straw in her drink. "But how did a working man like you score a Porsche? I'm *dying* to know."

"My uncle left it to me in his will. He died last year."

"Oh, I'm sorry. Were you close?"

"Yes—he taught me everything I know about racing." His face pinched up for a moment. "I could sell it—I sure need the money. But driving in it reminds me of him. I wouldn't sell that for the world."

I know what you mean, Jo thought, her heart going out to him.

"Enough about me," Antonio began, understandably anxious to change the subject. "I've been meaning to ask you—how'd you learn to speak Arabic?"

"Huh?" she asked, taken aback. "Wh-why do you want to know *that*?"

"I overheard you telling Jonathon you spoke Arabic, and I don't remember Sandra saying you did. So I was just wondering how you picked it up."

She crossed her fingers under the table and took a deep breath. "Well, um, my father had this oil baron friend from Saudi Arabia who stayed with us for a while when I was little," she fibbed. "So I guess that's where it started. And I studied it a bit in college. I'm not exactly fluent, though."

He raised his eyebrows. "Whoa, I'm impressed. Your dad must have friends in high places."

"My dad is dead," she said automatically, looking down. She hoped this true confession wouldn't blow her cover.

He touched her elbow. "I'm really sorry."

"It's okay."

"Well, I'm still sorry," he said quietly. "Listen, could we meet for coffee some weekend?"

"What?" she asked, heart racing. "I mean, um, sure."

"So how can I get in touch with you?" he asked.

"The Ritz," she said. "Uh, with my aunt— Camilla Stevens." Inside she kicked herself for giving up her home base so easily. But what could she do? Antonio had a way of getting her guard down. Besides, one coffee date wasn't going to hurt anything.

"Stevens?" he asked. "I thought your last name was Sanchez."

"It is," she stammered, "but it's my aunt from my mom's side."

He nodded and looked at his watch. "Oh no—I was supposed to meet my friend Graham at the gym ten minutes ago. I totally forgot today's our gym day."

She smiled. "That's okay—go."

"I hate to, believe me, but he'll kill me if I bail on him," he said apologetically. "I'll give you a call, okay?"

As he looked into her eyes she wondered if the strange feeling in her stomach was a product of excitement over this encounter or fear she was getting in too deep. Suddenly she couldn't tell the difference anymore.

That night at the suite Theresa paused for a moment over her French onion soup. "Was that a knock?" she asked.

Antonio! Jo thought, jumping to her feet and almost upending her salad. She floated to the door, her heart sinking a bit when she found only a bellman behind it. But her spirits lifted instantly when she saw he was holding a gigantic gold Godiva box.

"Package for a Ms. Natascia Sanchez," the man said.

"For me?" Jo cheered, grabbing the megabox out of his hands. She fished a few pound notes out of her pocket and blindly tossed them to the bellman.

"Very good, m'lady," he said, tipping his hat. "Have a pleasant evening."

Jo ripped open the card with glee. "Oh, my gosh, check this out," she demanded, heart rate accelerating faster than a zillion-horsepower engine. "'Natascia, here's to fast cars and faster friendships. Antonio.' Ohhh, couldn't you just *die?*"

"Pretty profound," Theresa said, focusing her gaze on the Godiva chocolates. "Pass 'em over."

"So how well do you know this guy?" Caylin asked. "Don't forget, Jonathon thinks a *translator* planted the bugs. And that more than likely means you, Jo. Maybe Antonio is one of Jonathon's cronies."

"Antonio has nothing to do with Jonathon," Jo said, rolling her eyes. Honestly, her roomie could be such a stick-in-the-mud. "I know him well enough, I assure you. Now which one should I have first? The pink one or the heart-shaped chocolate one?"

"Come on, you guys!" Caylin cried. "Jo's life could be in danger here. *All* our lives could be in danger now that this Antonio guy knows where we *are!* Doesn't that matter to you?"

"Not where chocolate's concerned," Theresa said as she studied the chocolate map. "Okay, Jo, you've got strawberry creme and macadamia nut. But—wait a second—the strawberry creme is supposed to be in the corner, not the middle."

"Same difference," Jo said, the pink confection just millimeters away from her mouth.

"Don't bite into it!" Theresa cried, batting the strawberry creme out of her hand.

"What are you doing?" Jo demanded. "Have you gone psycho or something?"

"No," Theresa said, pointing down to the map urgently. "See, these are all out of order. Which means they might have been *tampered* with."

"Hmmm. Can we say *par-a-noid*?" Jo quipped.

"You see? You see?" Caylin said, moving in for a closer look. "I bet Antonio *is* working with Jonathon. How can we be so sure he's not a bad guy?"

"Caylin's right. Look." Theresa held a piece of candy before Jo's eyes. "There's a little pinprick in the side here. And it looks like that's not the only one."

Jo inspected the candy herself, feeling a bit skeptical. But the more pinpricks she saw, the more convinced she became. "I guess we're better safe than sorry," she admitted.

"You'd better believe it!" Caylin ran her hand through her hair anxiously. "We should send these out to the lab immediately. Find out just what kind of guy we're dealing with here."

"I'll handle it," Theresa offered.

"And if there's *any* way you can convince them to *not* breathe a word of this to Uncle Sam, please do it," Caylin begged. "Because if he *ever* finds out that *someone* gave out our home base to a terrorist, that *someone's* going to get us all declassified!"

Jo shook her head in disbelief and flinched as Caylin's tirade sank in. Jo had let her friends down—and she'd let *herself* down, too. Clearly

Antonio was bad news from the beginning. Jo had known there was something different about him, something unnerving. Still, she couldn't believe that Antonio would actually want her dead. No way. Why would the guy who made her heart do back flips want to stop it from beating altogether?

10

"ey, Antonio," Jo called when she walked in the translation office on Thursday morning in her usual flirtatious fashion. "Thanks *so* much for the chocolates," she cooed. "I was just *super*tired last night, and I couldn't take a bite. But it was so sweet of you."

"Not at all," he said with a wink. "The pleasure is all mine, Natascia."

She shivered, wondering if she was only imagining the predatory flash in his eyes.

"Jo, William Nicholson needs your translating services ASAP," Sandra announced from her office. "It's urgent. He has someone in his office right now."

Oh no, she thought in a panic. Does he need my *Arabic* translating services? The color drained from her face as she headed to his office, feeling as if she was on her way to the electric chair.

When she entered the office, she found a well-dressed man sitting in front of Nicholson's desk. Please don't be Arabic, she chanted silently. Please don't be Arabic.

"Hello, Ms. Sanchez. This is Mr. Sandro from

Portugal," Mr. Nicholson said. "If you could kindly translate our conversation, it would be much appreciated."

"Certainly, sir," she said, breathing a big sigh of relief.

As the men began to talk she mindlessly translated the rather boring conversation between them. As far as she could tell, nothing of interest was being discussed—just a lot of political mumbo jumbo.

"Could we have a tour of the green room in the basement?" Mr. Sanchez asked in Portuguese, putting Jo on red alert.

Green room? she thought. Like, a perfect place for a *green* disk?

Nicholson cleared his throat after Jo translated the question. "Well, I can't discuss that with a translator present," he said, looking uncomfortable. "It's highly sensitive information."

The cat's got Nicholson's tongue, Jo realized, her heart soaring. This is the big break we've been waiting for!

"I have an amazing announcement," Jo told Caylin and Theresa the second she came through the door that evening.

"You've got a date with Liam Gallagher?" Theresa joked.

"No—how about you've found a good-tasting fat-free potato chip?" Caylin said, making a face as she bit into one from the open bag on her lap.

"Wrong and very wrong," Jo said, plopping down on the couch next to the girls. "I found out there's a green room in the embassy."

"A *what?*" Caylin and Theresa asked in stereo.

"A *green* room," she repeated. "I was clued in today while translating for Nicholson. Anyone else thinking what I'm thinking?"

"Green room, green disk?" Theresa said, eyebrows raised.

"Right on," Jo screeched, barely able to contain her excitement. "I mean, what are the odds? It's fate!"

"Hey, have you ever heard of the green room?" Caylin asked Fiona nonchalantly on Friday morning. Her pulse was racing in anticipation of getting the goods.

Fiona cocked her head thoughtfully. "I have heard of it but never actually seen it. And as far as I know, no one except for Mr. Nicholson himself is allowed down there."

"But do you know what's in there?" Caylin asked.

"No clue," Fiona said. "Confidential stuff—papers, documents, stuff like that. As far as I'm concerned, I'm glad it's off-limits. Just one more blasted room to clean."

Later that morning Caylin went back to the same storage closet where she'd found the date book. Even though she'd already turned it upside down, she figured it was worth another shot, like maybe Devaroux wrote out its location on a bottle of oil soap or something. She took all the bottles down from the shelves and inspected their labels closely but found nothing. Disheartened, she checked out the linen closet next.

"Uh, can I help you?"

She jumped and smiled cluelessly at the janitor hovering in the doorway. "Just looking for some bleedin' ammonia—you got any?" she asked, scratching her head.

"Try storage down the hall," he said, looking at her as if she were two sandwiches short of a picnic. "This closet's just for linens, hence the name."

"Sorry, fella," she said apologetically. "I'm new and all."

"Don't worry yourself, luv."

"Say—you know where the green room is?" she asked, deciding to take a chance. "That's something else I'm having trouble finding."

"Worked here three years, and I never heard of it," he said. "The green room, is it?"

"Yeah . . . well, maybe I sussed it wrong," she lied, her spirits plummeting. "Ta."

"Dinner reservations, eight o'clock sharp," Theresa announced the second she walked into suite 1423.

"Dinner reservations?" Jo asked. "Is that a good idea with this chocolate scare and all?"

"I took a call this afternoon confirming Jonathon

Nicholson's reservation for two at eight o'clock at Simpsons-in-the-Strand restaurant," Theresa said, chest swelling with pride over her coup. "Which means we now have instant dinner plans."

"Could be a good lead," Caylin said optimistically. "But sadly, I have nothing to wear." She put the back of her hand to her forehead and swooned dramatically.

"Cay's right, you know," Jo replied. "Jonathon knows what we look like. We have to go totally incognito. Does London have any after-hours wig shops?"

"Already taken care of," Theresa said. "If you'll head into my room, ladies, I believe you'll find a shipment of goodies from a designer I just *happen* to know personally. To my room, pronto!"

Jo and Caylin ran into Theresa's room lickety-split. Theresa followed behind, chuckling.

"All right, Mom clothes!" Jo cheered as she ripped open the box. After the chocolate scare Jacqueline Hearth's wacky fashions were just what the doctor ordered.

Caylin rubbed her hands together anxiously, looking like a kid on Christmas morning. "Bring 'em on!"

"This is too cool!" Jo cried, checking out the rainbow of vinyl clothes, fluorescent wigs, and feather boas.

"I can't believe your mom actually made these," Caylin said in awe.

"I have to admit, she *is* a splendiferous designer, even if her funky clothes don't exactly float my boat," Theresa admitted. "And Mom was hoping we'd road test these before she debuts them on the runway."

"Wow—what an honor!" Jo said, pink wig covering her black locks. She felt curiously carefree as she admired the colors, textures, and fabrics. "How did you get 'em here so quickly?"

"Mom's got a boutique here in London, so she arranged to have her samples messengered over today," Theresa explained.

"What do you think of these?" Caylin asked, pointing to the large cat-eye glasses perched on her nose. "Nonprescription."

Theresa laughed. "*Très* chic." She leaned over and grabbed a chartreuse boa from the stack. "How about this?" she asked, rolling her eyes as she wrapped it around her neck. "Is it me?"

"Oh, definitely," Jo gushed, chuckling. "Watch out, world—because the Spy Girls are glamming up tonight!"

"No way will Jonathon Nicholson recognize us under all this glitz and glimmer," Caylin chirped as she balanced a vinyl poor boy cap on top of a towering bouffant wig.

Well, one thing's for sure—we'll get noticed, Theresa mused as she checked out her too flashy reflection in the mirror. *And if* Jonathon *notices us, will he end up* recognizing *us, too?*

* * *

As Caylin entered Simpsons-in-the-Strand she almost burst out laughing. The restaurant was totally pretentious—huge abstract mural on the wall, well-coiffed diners in black clothes, tiny entrées on big plates with bigger price tags. It could have just as easily been in L.A. or New York—places like this were all the same. And they were definitely going to knock this one on its ear!

"May I help you?" the snooty hostess inquired, looking them up and down sourly.

"Reservation for three. Stevens," Jo replied, her tone just as stuffy as the hostess's expression.

"Yes," she said, giving them one more sweeping glance. "Right this way."

As they followed the hostess across the restaurant Caylin felt as though every person in the room had turned to watch them being seated. "Maybe we overdid it," she whispered, feeling a bit exposed in her pink wig, white vinyl dress, and pink platform boots.

"I don't think so," Jo said, shaking her cherry red wig and smoothing out her matching red vinyl jumper.

"Well, I for one feel like a Slip 'N Slide from third grade," Theresa joked, obviously referring to her bright yellow vinyl pants, matching baby T, and white Marilyn Monroe wig.

"Hey—there he is. Three o'clock." Caylin motioned slightly to a table for two in the corner where Jonathon was getting cozy with a striking redhead.

Theresa immediately started snapping pictures

with the special salt-and-pepper-shaker cameras she had whipped out of her bag and placed on the table. "What's our next move?" she asked. "Maybe we should send two drinks to Jonathon's table anonymously, only we bug the glasses first."

"I don't know," Caylin began, her heart pounding. "After what happened the other day, I think Jonathon's got his back up about this bugging thing."

"Not to worry—I've got the power accessory of the day, ladies." Jo waved a large, garish-looking costume ring under Caylin's nose. "It's really a long-range audio surveillance device. All I have to do is aim it in their direction and voilà."

"But how are we supposed to hear anything?" Caylin asked.

"The audio feeds straight into this." She pulled back a few wisps of cherry red "hair" to reveal an elaborate jeweled earpiece. "It's hideous, I know. Thank goodness it's hidden by the wig."

"Yeah, The Tower *is* kind of behind in the style department," Caylin said with a laugh.

"May I take your order?" a tall, waifish waitress inquired.

"We need a few minutes," Theresa requested.

The waitress departed, and Jo's brow wrinkled in concentration. "I'm starting to get a feed," she whispered. "Okay. It's working."

Caylin leaned over excitedly. "Are they talking about the disk?"

"Has he noticed us?" Theresa whispered, feeling like a sitting duck in her bright yellow ensemble.

"Give me a second," Jo admonished, putting her finger to her lips. She smiled. "Well, she *is* someone special."

"A coconspirator?" Caylin guessed. "A secret love?"

"Alfred's wife?" Theresa blabbed, shrugging as everyone turned to give her blank stares. "Well, he could have a wife, you know."

"Wrong on all counts. She's an old friend from high school who just arrived in London for a fellowship."

"Think it's a cover-up?" Caylin asked, eyeing the woman suspiciously.

"Highly unlikely," Jo said. "They're talking about old times—the prom, homeroom teachers, stuff like that. I think she's legit."

Theresa ran her hands through her wig frantically, sending it slightly off-kilter. "You mean I got dressed in this getup for nothing?"

Caylin smiled. "I happen to like this look and the fact that we're out together. So we went on a hunch and were wrong—big deal! At least we'll get some good eats out of the bargain."

"True and true again," Theresa agreed. "Now get that waitress over here. I'm a starvin' Marvin, and the chocolate mousse on that dessert tray has been taunting me."

Caylin's eyes wandered around the restaurant. Suddenly she spotted a familiar brunette parked at the far end of the bar. Short Hair! Their disguises weren't fooling anyone after all.

"Jo and T., there—at the bar—Short Hair!"

Caylin whispered, pointing to the far end, where only a half-full glass and an empty bar stool sat. "Darn!"

"Where?" Theresa said. "*The* Short Hair? I don't see her."

"She was right there," Caylin insisted, her nerves jangling. "Let me go look around."

Caylin did a tour of duty around the restaurant but returned a few minutes later, defeated. "She's nowhere to be found. Maybe she's the one who sent Jo the chocolates. Like, she's working with Antonio or something."

Jo's face fell. "No, I'm pretty much convinced that this woman is involved with Jonathon. And if she knows we're here, then *he* might know we're here."

"At this point I think it's safe to assume everyone's involved with everyone," Theresa suggested. "Let's blow this joint. I'll choose personal safety over chocolate mousse, no matter how painful the decision."

When they arrived back at the hotel after grabbing fish-and-chips at the neighborhood pub, the labs were awaiting them.

"Well, it was lucky you didn't eat those chocolates, Jo," Theresa said as she inspected the fax from The Tower lab.

"What is it?" Jo asked. "Not a love potion, I'm guessing."

"It turns out the chocolate was full of an elaborate chemical concoction dominated mainly by benazathol, kyryzalophin, and phyloranine. A signature cocktail—the kind of thing only used by spies and terrorists. Your average joe couldn't get this kind of thing on the street . . . or even on this side of the world."

"What would it have done to me?" Jo whispered, trembling.

"It would have paralyzed you at first, then worked almost like a truth serum. But three hours after you ingested it, you would have been dead."

"Oh, my gosh." Jo's blood chilled to below freezing. "Death by chocolate. For real." Tears welled up in her eyes. She'd come so close. . . .

Theresa wrapped her in a hug. "Hey, I was going to eat them, too, remember?"

"But you didn't, and that's what counts," Caylin said. "Listen, these people are playing for keeps. They don't care who they hurt to come out on top. And if we let them walk all over us, we should just hang this gig up right now. I, for one, am *not* going to allow that to happen. Are you with me?"

"I am," Theresa vowed.

Jo gulped as an image of her father flashed before her eyes. "Count me in," she said, her resolve strengthening. She wasn't going to let anyone walk on her again—especially not Antonio. And on Monday she was prepared to hit him with the cruelest joke she could play on him—surviving.

"Antonio, you devil, you," Jo cooed as she leaned against his desk first thing on Monday morning. He looked up at her and half gasped. She could practically feel the shock radiating off him.

"N-Natascia, hi," he stammered. "What's up?"

"Oh . . . not much," she insisted. "I just have some great news for you."

"And what is that, exactly?" he asked, his expression darkening.

"I finally tried those chocolates you gave me," she said, running a finger up his arm. "I wolfed down *every single last one* of them. All by my lonesome. Mmmm . . . they really were yummy to my tummy."

"Uh, that's . . . great," he muttered. His jaw sagged a little bit to the left.

"Thanks again, sweetie." She winked at him and sauntered over to her cubicle. There. Things were out in the open now. Seeing the look on his face made her brush with death almost totally worth it. She wished she knew what he was thinking now. He was probably going nuts trying to figure out who she was, what she knew, and why she hadn't perished from his spiked sweets. Probably questioning his masculinity or something, too.

Feeling empowered, Jo began sifting through the file cabinets in the office for info about the green room. She'd avoided the files thus far for fear of being caught. But today was the day to live on the edge. Finally, after searching through three full filing cabinets, she discovered a Spanish file marked *verde*. As she opened it slowly her heart nearly jumped in her throat. There, *en español*, were all the vital green room stats.

Jo, looking around the room to make sure she wasn't being watched, smiled triumphantly and slipped the document in her purse. She was going to find that disk before Antonio did, even if she had to die trying. She'd come close enough already.

As soon as Caylin and Theresa arrived at the Ritz on Monday evening Jo immediately sat them down on the living room floor. "Brace yourselves," she said. "I hit pay dirt."

Caylin held her breath. "What'd you find?"

"This," Jo said, extracting a piece of paper from her pocket. "*En español*. Green room vitals. How many entrances the floor has, its exact location, and—presto!—the company who installed the security system."

Theresa's mouth dropped open in disbelief. "Ohmigosh, it's too good to be true!"

"Rock on!" Caylin cheered. "This could be the key to finding our disk!"

"So what do we do next?" Jo asked, rubbing her hands together.

Theresa drifted away in thought for a moment. "I know. One of us should call to confirm the green room's security system ASAP. Once we've gotten that info, we move from there."

"Hello, this is Verna Frazier," Theresa announced in a nasal voice on Tuesday morning. "I'm an insurance clerk for the U.S. Embassy, and I need to confirm some security information."

"Okay, let me connect you with someone who can help you," said the Securitech receptionist.

Theresa's heart was practically pounding out of her chest, but she hoped her nervousness wasn't detectable over the phone lines. From the red phone booth in which she was huddled, she had a perfect view of the embassy across the street. The disk is somewhere in there, she thought, exhaling deeply. She didn't take her eyes off the building until someone picked up the line.

"This is Naomi Thompson. How may I assist?"

"Yes—this is Verna Frazier," Theresa said, making sure her voice sounded as nasally as it had before. "I'm an insurance clerk for the U.S. Embassy. I'm updating my files and need to confirm some security information."

"What sort of information?" the woman asked, sounding suspicious.

Theresa bit her lip and looked down at the handwritten piece of paper Jo had given her. "Let's see," she said, scanning the page. "It looks like I just need to confirm that the system in the green room is still the AC-Twenty, that there's a uniformed security guard employed twenty-four hours a day, and that the only person with authorized security clearance is William Nicholson, U.S. Ambassador."

"And *who* are you again?" the woman asked.

Theresa clutched the receiver a little tighter, knuckles whitening. "Verna Frazier," she repeated quickly, panic rising in her throat. "I'm an insurance clerk at the U.S. Embassy. I actually just started last week. The woman who had the job before me left the files in a wreck, and I have to turn in these reports this afternoon. So if you could help me, I'd really appreciate it."

"Certainly, ma'am," the woman said after a slight pause. "I can check that for you. Hold, please."

As Muzak filled her ears Theresa took a deep breath. Please don't let her come back and bust me, she thought, crossing her fingers.

"Okay," the woman said, returning. "The AC-Twenty and the security guard parts are correct, but the clearance is not. Mr. William Nicholson has full clearance, and it says here the cleaning crew has limited access Thursday nights from eight to ten in the evening."

Cleaning crew! Theresa thought, her spine

tingling. Looks like they're going to have some replacements this week!

"You wouldn't happen to have the name of that cleaning crew listed there, would you?" Theresa asked, attempting to sound as off-the-cuff as she possibly could. "I should probably call to confirm a few things with them—how many are in the crew, how it's invoiced, et cetera."

"Oh, sure," the woman said, totally buying Theresa's whole clueless-new-clerk act. "It's Sunbeam Cleaning Company down Hollyview Road. They're top-notch. They pretty much handle all the high-security jobs in town."

Theresa quickly scrawled the magic words on her piece of paper, then thanked the woman profusely. "You've really saved my day," she said with a laugh, "and maybe even my *life*."

"No problem at all," the woman said, chuckling modestly. "Have a smashing day."

Once I figure out how we can pass for the cleaning crew, Theresa thought, my day won't just be smashing—it'll be superfly.

"Yes, I'd love to work for Sunbeam," Caylin told the director of personnel at Sunbeam in her *Louise* voice before she left for the embassy. It wasn't the first call she'd made that Wednesday morning; she'd already called to cancel Sunbeam's Thursday night green room appointment in her *real* voice. "I hear you have a really nice outfit there, and I'm a real cleaning pro with oodles and oodles of references."

"Well, you're certainly an enthusiastic one now, aren't you?" he asked wryly. "How is one o'clock today?"

"That's brilliant," Caylin said, using the word that Brits seemed to use for everything and anything. "See you then."

The second she hung up the phone, Caylin was hit by the fact that she was supposed to be cleaning offices for Fiona at the same time she was going to interview for the Sunbeam cleaning job. And taking a late lunch wouldn't work since that wouldn't give her enough time to get everything to the seamstress and counterfeiter Uncle Sam had hooked them up with the night before. She scratched her head and racked her brain. How in the heck was she supposed to be in two places at the same time?

"Fiona, I'm really sick as a dog," Caylin said, doubling over her cleaning bucket from imaginary cramps at 12:38 P.M. "It's that time of the month, you know."

Fiona fixed her with a glare. "I've worked here five years, and I've only called in sick once. Once! And that's when I had gallstones."

"Well, unless you want this bucket filled with puke, I'm going to have to go," Caylin said, making her voice weak and feeble. "And I filled in for that girl who called in sick on bank holiday, remember? So give me a break."

Fiona's features softened a tiny bit. "Righty now,

I remember. Well, if you're sick, you're sick. Just leave me the list of which offices you haven't gotten to, and I'll see you tomorrow."

"So your references are clearly excellent, and we'd love to have you on board," Joseph Winslow, director of personnel at Sunbeam Cleaning Company, announced an hour later.

Caylin smiled brightly, thrilled he had bought her "hardworking Brit looking for extra dough" tale of woe. She was getting good at this acting stuff, if she did say so herself. If she kept this up, there could even be an Oscar somewhere in her future.

"You must be smiling in anticipation of seeing the lovely uniforms," Joseph joked. "Follow me and we'll get you set up."

"Do you chaps have photo ID cards as well?" Caylin asked.

He nodded. "Yes, but you won't need that until your first day on the job."

Caylin bit her lip. She really needed that ID card *today*. She walked along in silence for a moment, collecting her thoughts. After a few paces she said, "I know this sounds silly, but is there any way I could get my ID card today? I'm getting braces on Monday and would hate to have to look at a tin grin on my ID day in, day out. And I plan to be here for a long while, so it'd boost my morale to be able to have a picture I could be proud of." Even Caylin had a hard time keeping a straight face for that explanation.

Joseph looked at her as if she were a few cards short of a deck. "Braces?" he asked. "But your teeth are perfect."

Since she'd already endured two years of braces, he was right—they *were* perfect. She stuck her top teeth out a bit and tried not to smile. "Well, they look okay now, but my dentist says they're shifting. Happens to a lot of people, more than you'd think."

Joseph nodded as they entered the uniform closet. "Hmmm—well, I *guess* it's okay. As long as you don't say anything to anyone."

"My lips are sealed," she promised, locking her lips with her fingers and throwing away the imaginary key. "So these are the uniforms?"

"Straight off the runway," he joked. They were even drabber than the one she had to wear at the embassy. The ensemble consisted of navy blue polyester pants, a navy cotton smock that had a Sunbeam Cleaning patch above the left breast, and a matching Sunbeam Cleaning ball cap. *Gag.*

"I need a size . . ." She trailed off, trying to remember what a size eight was in Britspeak. "Thirty. Yes, a thirty." She sighed and thanked her lucky stars she wouldn't have to wear this outfit for more than one evening. Life's too short to wear polyester pants—that had always been her motto.

After he issued her uniform, Joseph snapped

her photo and laminated it to a blue-and-white ID card. "Okay," he said, "you're all set until Monday. See you at nine A.M. sharp."

In your dreams, she thought, but instead said with a tin-free smile, "See you then. Ta ta!"

Once she left the building, Caylin immediately fished her pressed powder compact cell phone out of her purse to call Uncle Sam, as he'd instructed.

"Go to room thirteen eleven in the Sullivan Suites at fourteen twenty-five Plumbtree Road in half an hour," he told her. "There a seamstress and counterfeit ID maker will be waiting. Good luck."

As she snapped the compact shut Caylin hoped—in light of their upcoming green room invasion—that they wouldn't be needing any *more* luck from here on out.

"Theresa, would you be a dear and run by the stationery shop after work to pick up my order?" Ms. Dalton asked her near the end of the day. "Then you could just bring it to work with you tomorrow morning."

"No problem," Theresa said with a smile. After all, it was the first time Dalton had ever asked her to do anything outside of the office and the woman was *way* too old to be trekking around town fetching supplies.

However, once she started making her way to the store, a huge knot formed in the pit of

Theresa's stomach. She was certain she was being followed. She kept looking over her shoulder warily, scared to death of what she might find behind her. Each time she saw nothing suspicious. But she still couldn't shake the eerie sensation.

She walked into the stationery shop and picked up Ms. Dalton's order without once experiencing that I'm-being-watched feeling. Her spirits lifted until she exited the store. Rain tore down in sheets all around her. Great, she thought. She was only about ten blocks from the Ritz and was wearing a raincoat, but she had no umbrella. So she stuck the sack in her raincoat pocket and made a mad dash for the tube, where at least she'd keep dry the two stops to the hotel.

A train pulled up immediately, and Theresa sank down into a seat. But as soon as the doors closed, that knot formed in her stomach again. This time, tighter.

She looked around at all the other passengers, checking to see if anyone's eyes were on her. One man met her gaze full on and held it a beat too long, totally giving Theresa the willies. How come only the wackos give me the eye? she wondered. Disgusted, she stood up to change cars.

She checked the reflections in the windows as she walked. Sure enough, Mr. Shifty had gotten up as well. He shuffled along behind her. Theresa's heart raced with fear. She sped up and bolted into the next car. When she glanced over her shoulder for a split second, she saw that he had sped up, too.

She dashed through the car, bumping into people along the way. When she looked back again, she noticed a bulge at the man's waistline that could only be a gun.

"That man pinched me!" she screamed. "He pinched me!" She pointed at the guy in anger, still keeping up her pace. She heard a few people call him a pervert, but that was it. She decided to go for the sympathy vote and employ an English accent in the next car. Even if that blew her cover with Mr. Shifty, she didn't care. She was running for her life now.

"That bloke pinched me on the bum!" she hollered the moment she opened the door to the next car. "Somebody help me! Please!"

As she ran down the aisle she glanced back and saw a group of rugby players stand in his path. But straight ahead she saw that the next car was the last. A dead end—in more ways than one. What was she supposed to do now?

She stepped out and stood between the two cars, the wet underground air tossing her hair about her face. Theresa shot a glance back at Mr. Shifty. He had made it halfway through the crowded car—only a few scant yards, one train door, and one very chivalrous rugby player separated them. Biting her lip, Theresa studied her surroundings. She had two options: get trapped in the next car or surf the top of the train. Either way you slice it, I could definitely croak, she thought. Her heart was racing so fast, she feared it was going to burst out of her chest. But she couldn't just stand by and make herself an easy target.

As she stole one last glance at her assailant she sighed deeply. "Here goes nothing," she muttered. She boosted herself up on the safety chain connecting the two cars and placed her hands on the top of the last car, her adrenaline pumping. Gathering all her strength, she pushed off the chain with her legs and hoisted her body on top of the car in one swift motion. She was almost immediately blown away—literally—by the whooshing wind in the tunnel.

I'm gonna die, she thought. Her sweaty palms, coupled with the condensation on the outside of the train, were making it almost impossible to keep her grip. Her fingers slowly slipped from their hold. Just when she thought she couldn't hold on even one second longer, Theresa glanced up—and spotted a dim light up ahead in the tunnel. A stop! she realized. If I can only hold on until then, I can make it!

The few seconds felt like an eternity. Please let me live, she prayed desperately, and I'll never pull anything this stupid again.

Suddenly the brakes engaged. Theresa flew forward, and her grip strained under the pressure. She held on for dear life as the train ground to a halt in the station. Her body began sliding to the left.

"You're almost there," she whispered, even though she knew her hardest move was yet to come. If she got off the train too soon, there was a chance Mr. Shifty would see her and snatch her. But if she tried to get off too late, she could get killed trying to jump off a moving train.

Once the doors slid open and she heard, "Please mind the gap," she held her breath and went for it. She scooted over to the side of the car, made her body go limp, closed her eyes, and rolled onto the concrete just as the doors whooshed shut.

As she hit the ground relief flooded her body. Taking a deep breath, she opened her eyes—and stared straight into the eyes of Mr. Shifty, now trapped behind closed doors.

She gasped. A look of disbelief overtook his sinister features, and he began to claw at the window desperately. As the train pulled out of the platform Theresa dragged herself up and gave her predator a "So there!" wave until he was no longer in sight.

"So then I jumped off the train and escaped," Theresa relayed to Uncle Sam via videophone just moments after returning to suite 1423. Although she was bursting with pride, the train adventure had definitely left her shaky.

Neither Jo nor Caylin looked as if they could believe what Theresa had just been through. But while Caylin's face beamed with pride, Jo looked upset and concerned.

"First, I want to commend you on how you handled yourself, Theresa," Uncle Sam said. "You weighed your options, relied on your instincts, and did what you had to do. Good job."

Theresa smiled. "All in a day's work."

Uncle Sam chuckled. "Second, you need to be on high alert with the conference coming up in just four days," he continued, his voice suddenly grave. "You've given me a good description of your would-be attacker and I'll get an artist on the composite. In the meantime don't open your hotel doors to anyone. Look around when you're walking outside. Be aware of your surroundings. The stakes are getting higher, and these people don't care who they have to crush to get what they're after. So beware."

"We'll be extra careful, Uncle S.," Caylin promised. "We're crossing our fingers that the disk is in the green room and that it will be in our hot little hands mañana.

Uncle Sam cleared his throat. "I hope so, too. But in the event that it's not there, I'm confident you'll recover it somehow."

Theresa wished she could say the same. She wasn't so sure she could anymore.

This polyester is going to give me hives!" Caylin whispered as the trio made their way to the green room at 8 P.M. sharp Thursday evening in their custom-made Sunbeam uniforms.

As they approached the tall, wiry guard he eyed them curiously. "You aren't the ones who usually come," he said in a suspicious tone, looking them up and down.

"We're the fill-in crew," Caylin said, as they'd rehearsed. According to Theresa's plan, Caylin was to do all the talking. "Thomas, Martha, and Hugh were on a long-distance assignment and got held up, so we've been sent in their place."

She presented her ID card, and Jo and Caylin followed suit. "Well, I didn't hear anything about this, and there are strict policies," the security guard said. "Perhaps I'll just call your HQ."

"Go right ahead," Theresa said, keeping her cool only because she'd had the foresight to have Sunbeam's calls forwarded to The Tower just fifteen minutes earlier.

As he dialed the digits Theresa's hands began to shake slightly. The operator had said the phone calls would be transferred within ten minutes—but what if there was a delay?

"Yes," the security guard said into the phone, "this is James at the U.S. Embassy. I'm just calling to verify that in lieu of our regular crew being held up, you've sent over a Ms. Frazier, Ms. Hanover, and Ms. Fineberg."

He paused and looked them over closely. Theresa took another deep breath. "Okay, I see." He nodded. "Oh, they did?" When he scratched his eyebrow and smiled over at them, Theresa figured they must be home free. "Very well, then. Have a good evening."

He hung up and smiled at them apologetically. "Sorry about that," James said, his tone a million times nicer. "Policy, you know."

Caylin shrugged. "We understand."

"Just let me buzz you in here," he said, punching some numbers into a keypad. The steel door raised up, allowing them entry. "This door will automatically close behind you. It will open again at ten o'clock sharp. If you need anything, press the red button and I'll buzz myself back in. Otherwise I'll see you at ten."

Caylin's heart sped up as she followed the guard into the green-walled room, equipped with four desks, four computers, four fax machines, six ten-line phones, four paper shredders, and six huge filing cabinets.

As soon as the steel door closed behind them they sprang into action. "Okay, you know what to do. And remember: Leave no surface unturned," Caylin whispered, dashing to a desk and exploring every crack and crevice.

Jo and Theresa followed Caylin's lead, beelining to the two desks on the opposite end of the room. "So should we only get the green disks?" Jo asked in confusion.

"Grab every disk you can, no matter what color," Theresa said. "The 'green' was probably just a reference to this room."

Caylin dug through a drawer like a puppy digging for a bone. As she found disk after unmarked disk her spirits lifted considerably. She knew that going through them later would be time-consuming and that maybe Devaroux had even planted a file in a file, but it felt good holding them in her hands.

"We have too much ground to cover," Jo complained. "I don't think we'll have enough time!"

"No whining—we'll find it," Caylin said, not looking up. She had tunnel vision at the moment and was focused on nothing more than recovering the disk. This was how she felt when she hang-glided or snowboarded—totally centered and determined to be all she could be. And that's what she was trying to do in the green room, for the sake of the mission and the fate of the world.

"We'd better start cleaning up," Caylin announced suddenly. "It's nine-forty. We've only got twenty minutes."

"Ohmigosh!" Theresa cried in disbelief. She went into a tailspin of activity, putting the room back together as frantically as she had torn it apart. By 9:58 the room looked immaculate and the duffel bag Caylin had smuggled in was full to bursting with floppies.

"Anyone need to wipe her brow?" Theresa asked as Jo and Caylin struggled to replace a computer monitor they had searched under. Theresa reached into a box of Kleenex, her fingers brushing something hard, flat, and very familiar feeling. She yanked the object out of the box and screamed with excitement. "Check this out! A green disk! A *green disk!*"

Jo and Caylin froze in place and gaped, open-mouthed, the monitor still in their hands.

"This was hidden in the Kleenex box!" Theresa exclaimed. "This is it!"

Jo and Caylin jumped up and down as Theresa kissed the disk in sheer glee.

The door whooshed open and James stepped inside. "Okay, it's ten o'clo—oy, what in blazes is going on in here?"

Jo shrieked. Caylin gasped. Theresa looked on in horror as they flung the monitor away from them. It hit James squarely in the gut. His eyes went wide with shock and he fell backward.

"Look out!" Theresa screamed, but it was too late. James hit his head on the edge of a desk with a sickening *thunk* and sank to the floor.

"Wha-what?" he muttered, giving the girls a

last, dazed once-over before passing out cold.

"Is he still breathing?" Theresa squeaked. She clutched the duffel bag, terrified.

Caylin bent down over him. "Yep." She shrugged. "Well, this is our out. Let's book!" She led the mad dash down the hall and began frantically pushing the elevator button.

"What's wrong?" Jo cried desperately. "Open, stupid doors, open!"

"It's after ten," Caylin said. "The doors probably won't work."

"There's a secret door here somewhere," Jo recalled. She strained her brain but couldn't remember the floor plan. "Let's just push all the tiles. Maybe something will give."

Caylin pushed as hard as she could against the tiles on the opposite side of the hall, frustrated. "This isn't getting us anywhere. Maybe they tiled over the secret door or something."

"Oh n-no," Theresa stammered. "I think James is coming to." Her eyes were glued down the hall at the guard's twitching foot. She looked as if she might puke. "H-Hurry up, guys."

Jo pushed tile after tile after tile until finally she felt one give. A satisfying whoosh at her feet heralded the opening of a two-foot-high hatch. "I've got it!" she called proudly. Without even thinking, she jumped in. She immediately regretted it as she slid toward oblivion in a coffin-wide metal chute.

Chilled to her core, Jo screamed in the hopes

of saving her friends from suffering the same. But her cry was quickly joined by Caylin's wail and Theresa's squeal. They plunged toward certain death, their voices raised in a chorus—metallic, echoing, and terrifying. The sound plucked Jo's spine with cold fingers. Desperate, she reached out and tried to grab onto the sides of the chute, but the metal was more slippery than an oil slick.

Jo closed her eyes and prayed the chute had an end . . . *somewhere*. Visions of the center of the earth and a bed of foot-high spikes danced in her mind. She screamed even louder, her heart nearly stopping from fear. She kept screaming and screaming until her echoing wail turned into no more than a flat screech. Suddenly she realized she wasn't moving anymore.

Jo opened her eyes and squinted into the darkness. She was lying on an old mattress. The room around her was totally bare—dirt floor, dirt walls. Jo stood up tentatively. She realized with a start that the screams behind her were growing louder. She stepped off the mattress and down came Theresa with a thump, followed by Caylin right on top of her.

"That rocked—in a really weird way," Caylin said.

"Oh, stop!" Theresa cried. "Don't even joke about that, Cay. For about three full minutes I swear I was watching my own funeral on the backs of my eyelids."

"Well, you can rest easy," Caylin remarked. "Now we just have to figure out where we are."

"I don't know—there's nothing here but dirt," Jo said. "Maybe it's just your basic, average secret room. Do you think this is still embassy property?"

Theresa cocked her head. "I don't know. I think we were moving more to the side than down, to be honest. Instead of taking us below the building, the chute shot us away from it."

Jo shrugged. "The architect must have had a wiggy sense of humor," she offered.

"No—this is probably a full-on escape hatch," Caylin pointed out. "Like in case of a terrorist attack."

"Well, I sure hope Jonathon Nicholson knows about it," Theresa said. "He's going to need it if we didn't get that disk."

"The disk!" Caylin gasped. "Theresa, do you—"

"I've got all of 'em right here," Theresa assured her, holding up the duffel bag.

Caylin sighed with relief. "Thank goodness. Now let's head down this passageway and find a way out of here." She dusted the soot off her polyester duds and grinned wryly. "At least we don't have to worry about getting our clothes dirty, right?"

"Caylin, I'm getting a bad feeling," Theresa complained. "Maybe we should sit down and rest. Or ... maybe ... fall ... asleep. ..."

"Oh, you've always got a 'bad feeling,'" Caylin griped. "Where's your sense of adventure?"

"I left it in the dryer too long," Theresa quipped. "It shrank."

Caylin chuckled, but inside she was torn. She had absolutely no idea where she was or where they all were headed. Every time she turned a corner, she expected to see Dracula or Freddy Krueger or even that weird white teddy bear from those fabric softener commercials. That thing always gave her the creeps. But she put her irrational fears aside and kept walking, kept leading, kept hoping with quickened pulse that she wasn't about to set foot in a trap.

"Jeez, this is making me tired," Theresa complained. "Have you noticed how exhausting this walk is? We've only been going about twenty minutes, and I'm pooped."

"Yeah," Jo agreed. "It's an uphill battle."

"It is!" Theresa snapped her fingers. "Guys, we're heading up. Slowly but surely. This tunnel will take us to ground level!"

Or maybe ground *zero*, Caylin thought with a wince. She hoped not. She hoped that wherever the tunnel took them, it had nothing to do with Jonathon, or Laqui Bay, or Godiva chocolates. She just wanted to get back to the Ritz, shimmy out of that itchy polyester, and sort through those disks, pronto.

Theresa sprinted past Caylin, supercharged by the fresh air blowing on her face. "We've made it!" she cried. "The end! We're safe!"

"Shhh! Don't push your luck," Caylin warned. "Just because the end of the line is outdoors doesn't mean it's not dangerous."

"I don't care," Theresa sassed, her lungs practically singing. "Oh, to be out of that musty tunnel . . . 'tis heaven." She reached the end of the line and stopped cold in her tracks, amazed by what she saw.

"What is it?" Jo cried.

"Are we safe?" Caylin hollered, hurrying to catch up. "Yell if you're in trouble!"

"I'm fine," Theresa said, dumbfounded. "It's just . . . that . . ."

"What?" Caylin reached Theresa's side and looked around. She gasped, her blue eyes widening. "I don't believe it."

"I don't get it," Theresa added.

"I don't even want to know," Jo chimed in as she reached the end of the line.

Theresa shook her head. She couldn't piece it all together. She and her partners, after a death-defying plummet down a chute and a never-ending walk through underground catacombs, were standing not on the threshold of an amazing discovery or a deadly trap. No, they were standing in the mouth of a large, defunct drainage pipe near the banks of the Thames. Totally alone. Totally confused. Totally ticked off.

"This has got to be the lamest payoff *ever*," Caylin groaned.

"I still don't get it," Theresa murmured, slinging

the duffel of disks over her shoulder. "Why even bother, you know?"

"Like I said before," Jo quipped, "that architect must have had one *wiggy* sense of humor."

After two hours of watching Theresa sit at her laptop and open every single file on every single disk, Caylin's anticipation had vanished into thin air.

The first defeat had come when their trump card, the green disk, turned out to be completely empty. Now, with every disk Theresa tested and eliminated, Caylin's frustration mounted to dangerous levels. *Maybe the heat coming off my head is screwing up the laptop,* she thought halfheartedly.

"This is the last one," Theresa said, holding up a red floppy. She stuck the disk into the drive and waited.

The ceaseless whirring of the disk drive made Caylin want to trash the suite rock-star style. Toss a few TVs out the windows, set stuff on fire, the usual. She'd never do it, of course. But it was fun to think about. More fun than listening to that darned whirring.

The whirring stopped. Caylin held her breath in anticipation until the dreaded prompt—*This disk is not initialized. Do you wish to initialize it now?*—appeared on-screen.

"Darn it," Theresa muttered.

Jo sighed. "I guess we wore polyester for nothing."

Caylin got up without a word and walked into her bedroom, slamming the door in defeat.

Friday night Jo sulked back to the Ritz after an uneventful day at work. Antonio was a no-show at the office, and Sandra had said he was sick. Sick in the *head,* Jo thought with a shudder. To make matters worse, Sandra had finally pigeonholed Jo into putting together the "up-tempo numbers" for the after-conference ball—on a *Sunday. Ugh!* What a way to spend the end of a weekend. *Especially* if it turned out to be the last weekend of her life.

A red Porsche approached the crosswalk, distracting Jo from her thoughts. What I wouldn't give to be in the front seat of that baby, Jo mused, hair flying everywhere, pedal to the metal, radio cranked to ten-point-five, no worries. To her surprise, the dream machine first slowed down and then completely stopped right in the middle of the road next to where she was standing.

As the tinted window came down she looked in, curious. One glance made her blood run cold: Antonio sat in the driver's seat. Jo took off running as fast as she could. She spotted an alleyway and ducked into it. But as she exited the alley and rounded the corner near the post office, she could see his car clearing a hill in the distance and coming her way. How were her size-seven feet supposed to compete with a Porsche?

Her eyes landed on a VW double-parked in front of the post office, motor running. Without a moment's thought Jo jumped in the VW and slammed her foot on the gas.

"It's not like I'm *stealing* it or anything," she told her reflection in the rearview mirror. She was simply *borrowing* it to escape Antonio, who was now hot on her trail. She made a sharp turn onto a busy side street and erratically swerved in and out of traffic, trying desperately to lose the chocolate poisoner. This wasn't just *any* chase. She was driving for her life. And on the wrong side of the street, too.

As she wove between vehicles Jo saw red lights flashing on and off in the distance. Jo squinted to make out the sign below them: Train Crossing.

"Oh no," she muttered, stepping on the gas even harder. That was all she needed—to be trapped behind a who-knows-how-long train with nowhere to run or hide. If that happened, she'd be dead in no time.

She looked back at Antonio and swore she saw him smiling. "You jerk!" she muttered. "I might be in a VW, but I can outdrive you any day of the week!"

She heard the engine chug slightly and looked down at the dash in alarm. "Engine—fine," she read aloud. "Pressure—fine. Gasoline—*empty?*" Goose bumps covered her arms as she realized she might not even have enough gas to make it across the tracks.

The black-and-white barriers were descending, and the flash of silver on the track was coming closer and closer. She looked down again at the gas gauge—below *E.* A glance in the rearview confirmed her worst fears—Antonio's Porsche was just inches behind. It was now or never time: Should she gun it and risk getting killed or brake and risk getting killed?

Jo held her breath, closed her eyes, and floored it. She felt the tracks bump under the wheels just seconds before she heard the train whoosh by, the brute force of its speed rocking the little VW. The engine coughed and sputtered, but she'd made it.

She opened her eyes and checked the rearview. Only a blur of silver could be seen—no Antonio. He was behind the train, eating her dust.

Trembling, she breathed a deep sigh of relief and turned down the nearest side street. Sputtering along, she was shocked to feel tears run down her cheeks. Tears of rage over Antonio's relentless pursuit. Tears for her father, who had been taken away before his time. And tears for the mission, which she feared might not be solved despite all the efforts of her and her friends. She wiped the tears away with the back of her hand, forcing herself to get it together. After all, she had gas to get, a car to ditch, a hotel to return to, and a major score to settle. There was no time to waste.

*   *   *

"So then I made sure I left no prints on the car and left it a few blocks away from the post office," Jo told Uncle Sam a few minutes after she'd arrived back at the Ritz, safe and sound.

"I can't believe you survived that," Theresa said, completely blown away.

"I can," Uncle Sam said. "The conference is only three days away, and things are coming to a head. With that in mind, Theresa—go to the fax machine right now. I'm sending a photo of someone I'd like you to identify."

Theresa ran to the fax machine, where a blurry black-and-white photograph was coming through on paper.

"Does this man look familiar to you?" Uncle Sam asked.

Theresa pulled the paper out of the machine and held it under the desk lamp. Her blood ran cold. "Ohmigosh—that's him! The guy who chased me on the train! But what—I mean, how—"

"Thanks to the description you gave me, this man was detained yesterday when he entered Heathrow under an alias. However, he somehow managed to escape custody when customs detained him for a passport check." He paused, and Theresa shook slightly. "We believe he's the infamous Alfred."

"Alfred?" Theresa repeated in disbelief. Not only had she escaped a madman on the train that day. The madman was also an international terrorist in cahoots with Jonathon!

"We believe he is Alfred, yes," Uncle Sam replied. "His passport was falsified, but when they searched the airport for him, he was nowhere to be found." Uncle Sam paused. "This means he could very well be in your neck of the woods, and judging by Antonio's actions, they might very well think you have the disk. You all could be in grave danger."

"I think I'm gonna be sick," Theresa said, hauling full speed to the bathroom. Before anyone could react, she was puking her guts out into the marble toilet. This is where our mission seems to be right now, she thought between hurls. Right down the toilet.

"Come out, come out, wherever you are, diskie," Caylin muttered as she combed through a filing cabinet Saturday afternoon. She'd had to scheme and scam to be able to fill in for the weekend cleaning woman, and at the very least she hoped her efforts would pay off.

But wherever she looked—under phones, through trash cans, in drawers—no disk. She even pulled out seat cushions in her mad search, but found only nada.

As Caylin glanced at her reflection in a nearby window she took a deep breath. She looked totally tired. And she *was* tired—tired of not finding the disk, of feeling inadequate, of doubting her abilities. She was used to savoring the thrill of victory, not choking down the agony of defeat.

Disheartened by Caylin's unsuccessful search, Jo dragged her feet back to the embassy on Sunday to finally perform her special music assignment. When Jo arrived, Sandra led her straight to the door marked Private—the one she had unsuccessfully tried to open her first day on the job. Jo was amazed that almost three weeks had passed since that day; she wasn't any closer to recovering the list of nuclear warheads than she had been then. The realization was beyond discouraging.

"Here's where all the CDs are kept," Sandra said as she unlocked the room. "You'll need to pull enough music for four hours—an hour and a half of dinner music, two and a half of dancing music."

When the door opened, Jo gasped. The room—maybe five feet by five feet—was wall-to-wall CDs. "Where did all these come from?" she asked. "It looks like a radio station in here!"

"That's what it is, sort of," Sandra said, laughing. "You'll notice all the CDs are marked with stickers saying Property of BLC, British Radio. That used to be Mr. Nicholson's radio station. He sold it to a chap a few years back, turned it into chat radio—you know, no music. So Mr. Nicholson donated the CDs to the embassy."

"Wow," Jo breathed, still in shock. As she marveled at all the CDs her awe suddenly turned to anguish as she realized there were probably hundreds of nooks and crannies such as this one the girls hadn't even checked yet, would maybe *never* get the chance to check. And time was running out.

Later that evening the girls sat on the floor of their suite, surrounded by every note and scrap of paper they'd accumulated over the past three weeks, totally at wit's end.

"What could we be missing?" Caylin asked as she picked up the green room stat sheet and stared at it in vain.

"It has to be right under our noses," Theresa said, raking her fingers furiously through her brown hair.

"But the question is—where?" Jo inquired. "There are probably a million places we haven't even looked at—"

The videophone rang, cutting Jo off. "Hold that thought," Caylin said, grabbing the TV remote and pushing talk. "Hello?"

"Uncle Sam here, ladies," he said, his voice accompanied by a black screen. "How are you holding up?"

"Not so good," Jo replied in a decidedly glum tone.

"Well, you've still got tomorrow," he reminded them. "You've been E-mailed the address of the FBI safe house, which is two blocks from the embassy. Go by there as soon as possible just so you know where it is. You're to report there at six P.M. sharp whether you've recovered the disk or not."

"But we don't want to go without the disk!" Jo cried.

"If you don't have it by six, you'll have to accept that sometimes a mission is successful simply because you survived it," he said. "But you can all rest easy knowing you've given it your best shot, no matter what happens."

Caylin sighed deeply. The sigh echoed hollowly

in her throat. She felt powerless, as if she'd just lost a kickboxing title. When she looked over at Theresa, she noticed tears were glistening in her eyes. Uncle Sam wished them the best of luck and signed off quickly.

"What are we going to do if we don't find it?" Caylin wondered aloud. "I can't handle failing at our first mission."

"Me neither," Theresa said. "We've passed so many tests along the way. It's hard to believe we might flunk the final."

"Especially when there's who knows how many places we haven't even had access to in that embassy," Jo said. "That's what I was going to tell you before Uncle Sam called. Today I had to go through the CDs in a little closet off the ballroom. That cubbyhole, which is pretty much locked twenty-four-seven, was a total reality check of how much of that embassy we probably haven't even explored."

Caylin took a deep breath. "Pretty discouraging, isn't it?"

"You can say that again," Theresa said. "But we're all worn-out. Maybe we'll feel fresher in the morning after a good night's sleep."

"You're right," Jo said, pulling herself up off the paper-covered floor. "I can't think about this another second."

"It's probably a good idea to get some rest," Caylin agreed. "It's going to be a big day tomorrow, no matter what."

* * *

A few minutes later Theresa shrieked loudly.

"What's wrong?" Caylin said, dashing into Theresa's room.

"Ohmigosh, what is it?" Jo screeched, hot on Caylin's heels.

"The CDs!" Theresa exclaimed, sitting straight up in her bed. "The ones you had to go through today."

"What about them?" Jo asked, looking perplexed.

"Compact *discs*, don't you see?" Theresa asked excitedly. "Maybe Frank wasn't referring to a floppy disk after all."

Caylin's eyes suddenly lit up. "Ohmigosh, could that be it?"

Jo smiled. "Could be."

"The only thing is," Theresa said, "how many CDs were there?"

"Like a thousand," Jo replied in a dejected tone. "How would we know which one to look in even if you *are* right?"

The girls fell silent for a moment.

"How about ones with *green* in the title?" Theresa asked, head spinning. "Like *Green*, by R.E.M., or the Jam's 'Pretty Green'?"

"Or the *Green Acres* theme!" Jo suggested with a laugh. "Or how about that wiggy old psychedelic song—you know, 'Green Tambourine'?"

"Green Day!" Caylin exclaimed, smiling hugely. "Or *Green Mind*, by Dinosaur Jr."

"Yeah!" Theresa clapped. "Or maybe that Kinks album—*The Village Green Preservation Society*!"

Jo and Caylin stared at her questioningly.

"Hey, my mom played that all the time when I was a kid." Theresa rolled her eyes. "Look, whatever, there are tons of possibilities." She smiled, her heart swelling with pride.

"Wait, how about CD covers that are green, too?" Jo asked. "That could be what he meant."

"Oh, that's good!" Caylin exclaimed. "I can hardly wait to get in there! What time could you get into the closet, Jo?"

"Sandra has to pick up some dignitaries, so she won't be in until around three," Jo said. "But we could meet there then. I'll just tell her I need to grab more music for the ball."

"Sounds like a plan!" Theresa sang, eyes shining with hope. This was the first time in a while she'd actually felt as if they could solve this sucker. And maybe her lead was going to be the one they'd been waiting for!

"Man, if this theory is right," Caylin said, "we're going to love you forever, Theresa."

"Well, I would have never come up with it if it hadn't been for Jo going there today," Theresa replied modestly.

"Wow—mutual admiration society!" Caylin laughed. "I guess that means we're a good team."

"You guys know that and I know that," Theresa said. "But I hope we get the chance to prove it to the world tomorrow."

O kay, so, Caylin, you go through the green CDs on the south wall, I'll take the north wall, and Theresa take the west wall," Jo instructed as she unlocked the door to the CD closet on Monday afternoon.

"Then we'll all go through the ones on the east wall, right?" Caylin asked.

"Yep," Jo replied, oozing with confidence. "And after that, if we still haven't found it, we'll go through the green names."

"But that could take a little longer since it's more abstract," Theresa noted. "And if all else fails, we'll just go through every single one until we find it."

When Jo opened the door, Caylin and Theresa gasped.

"Whoa," Caylin said, sounding overwhelmed.

"Whoa is right," Theresa said. "There's way more than a thousand CDs in here. More like *ten* thousand!"

"Really?" Jo asked, heart sinking. "I'm just horrible with numbers."

Caylin sighed. "It's okay, it's okay," she

murmured reassuringly. "We've just got to take it disc by disc and not look at the big picture. So let's do it!"

"This is a lost cause," Theresa muttered two and a half hours later, her hair sticking up every which way and little cuts from the sharp CD cover corners covering her fingers.

They'd already gone through all the discs with green covers and with *green* in a song or band title with no success and were now going through what was left in this, their final hour. CDs were flying everywhere, the room was a wreck, and claustrophobia was kicking in. Caylin and Jo looked discouraged, and Theresa was pretty much resigned to the fact that her hunch had been wrong after all.

A sudden pounding on the door made everyone jump. "Don't answer it—it could be Antonio," Jo whispered.

"Or Jonathon," Caylin added.

"Or Alfred," Theresa realized out loud, her blood running cold. She pushed the possibility aside and got back to brass tacks. "Are you totally sure we checked that R.E.M. CD, Jo? I can't believe it wasn't in there."

"Yeah, I'm sure," Jo said as the knocking grew more insistent.

"How about Green Day?" Theresa inquired. We must have overlooked *something,* she told herself. That disc has to be in here!

"Checked. I've got their CD right here," Caylin said, grabbing it off the filing cabinet. "Jeez, that knocking is *really* giving me a headache."

"Hey, that's not their only CD," Theresa said, motioning to the disc in Caylin's hand. "Where's the one with all the hits on it—I think it's called *Dookie?*"

"Ohmigosh," Jo breathed, gasping and looking up at the other girls in horror. "I pulled that one yesterday! Sandra has them. I totally forgot—she must have at least thirty CDs. We've got to find her!"

This news flash filled Theresa with pure adrenaline. "Okay, okay," she told the knocker in annoyance, swinging the door open swiftly. But she gasped in horror when she saw not one knocker but two—Antonio and Jonathon!

"Whoa!" Jo gasped, jumping back in shock. Before the fiends could react, she barreled past them, knocking them over, and ran top speed over to the other side of the ballroom. She began grabbing the CDs off the corner shelf.

"Natascia," Sandra demanded, "just *what* do you think you're doing?"

Jo threw some CDs Caylin and Theresa's way and led them out of the ballroom without a glance in Sandra's direction. Caylin and Theresa were hot on her heels—Jonathon and Antonio were hot on theirs.

"Who's got it?" Caylin yelled, running at light

speed toward the exit up ahead. "The Green Day?"

Her pace never faltering, Jo shuffled through the CDs and smiled as if she'd found Willy Wonka's golden ticket. "I got it!" she cheered. She separated it from the rest of the pile without slowing her pace or dropping CDs under her feet. Glancing back, she saw Antonio and Jonathon still in hot pursuit, their arms outstretched and ready to grab.

As she neared the exit doors Jo firmly grasped the Green Day CD in one hand, never slowing her pace for a second. "Okay, here goes," she said, voice trembling.

"Please be in there, please be in there," Theresa chanted, while Caylin went white as a sheet.

Jo held her breath as she opened the cover gingerly. And there, nestled inside, was a shiny CD-ROM reading *Classified* instead of *Dookie*.

The most beautiful sight I've ever seen, Jo thought.

Theresa pushed open the exit doors—and gasped as she ran smack-dab into a man's broad chest. And when she looked up, she discovered she'd bumped into not just any man but *Alfred.*

"Dirty rotten girl chaser!" she yelled, kicking him hard in the shins. "It's payback time!" As Alfred doubled over she took off running. Antonio and Jonathon were gaining in a major way.

Theresa ran into the street. A fast-approaching Fiat screeched to a halt and swerved, just barely missing her.

"Bloody idiots!" the driver screamed out the window, but Theresa didn't even stop to react. Not with Jonathon and Antonio so close behind.

"Have some CDs, guys!" Jo hollered, her right hand grasping the Green Day CD case tightly. She dropped the extras behind her. Theresa followed suit, as did Caylin, and discs flew everywhere. The clatter of plastic on concrete mocked Jo's frazzled nerves. The guys faltered, but they instantly regained their footing. Jo ran on without looking back, desperate not to lose hold of her precious cargo.

Caylin felt fingers brushing her back. She shot a look over her shoulder—Jonathon! He was trying to grab her!

Frantic, Caylin led him toward a phone booth. Her heart pounding with fear, she stopped suddenly, sending Jonathon rushing past her and into the booth. She kicked a trash can in front of the door. "Call nine-one-one," she taunted, her adrenaline overtaking her terror. "You need some major help!"

Caylin left him pounding on the door and ran toward the FBI safe house. She spotted Jo dashing up the sidewalk, the CD case held firmly in her right hand. Caylin poured on the heat to catch up, but she was knocked to the ground by a man in a dark coat who kept on running. Antonio!

"Jo! Look out!" Caylin yelled from the ground.

Jo looked over her shoulder, the action slowing her down a bit. Without a word Antonio pulled even and grabbed the priceless case out of her hand.

"I don't *think* so!" she screamed, tackling him to the ground. Her pulse pounding—from excitement or terror, she couldn't tell—she grabbed for the case in Antonio's hand.

"Hey! Over here!"

Jo looked up to see Caylin up and running and heading right toward her. Antonio did the same and relaxed his grip on the case. Propelled by sheer willpower, Jo yanked the case from his slimy hand. "I believe that belongs to *us*," she said, tossing the case to Caylin as hard as she could.

Caylin stretched out her fingers and reached for the flying case. Alfred lunged for it, too. Not fast enough. Caylin tripped him and made a successful snag. She exhaled in relief and pounded the pavement with all her might. The FBI safe house was only one block away. She was going to deliver the disc. She *had* to.

Jonathon, free from the phone booth, caught up to her. "Give—me—that," he demanded, sideswiping Caylin and hitting her hand. The case flew from her grasp.

The feeling of the case slipping through her fingers was the sickest she'd ever had. The sight of Jonathon grabbing it out of midair made her want to throw up. But she wasn't going to let that case get away. Her muscles vibrating with nervous energy, she chased Jonathon for a few feet, then—fueled by the sight of the safe house just two doors up—knocked him over with all her weight, sending the CD case flying and sending Jonathon into a cursing frenzy.

Caylin recovered the case from the gritty cement and ran like lightning to the safe house. She was halfway up the safe house stairs when Jonathon caught up to her and knocked the case out of her hands again, sending it flying onto the porch.

"Nowhere to hide, *Louise*," he crowed as he dashed past her.

Caylin heard tons of footsteps scrambling all around her, but her eyes never left the CD prize. Just as Jonathon dove for the disc an FBI agent swung open the screen door of the house, whacking him hard on the head.

With a roar of victory Caylin kicked the case out of Jonathon's grasp and into the house, where it skidded across the floor to safety.

"Put your hands up!" the agent commanded, leveling a gun in Jonathon's direction.

"Yeah, freeze, sucker!" Caylin cheered.

A look of confusion flashed on Jonathon's face. What's he so confused about? she wondered as he was cuffed and taken into the safe house. Surely he realized he ran the risk of being arrested before undertaking such an evil endeavor. Either that or he was a first-class idiot.

Theresa, struggling for breath, made it into the safe house and ran to Caylin's side. Her heart was nearly pounding out of her chest as Jo burst in seconds later, Alfred and Antonio hot on her heels.

Theresa sighed with relief when Alfred and Antonio were cuffed and taken into custody. She checked out the black-clad, totally professional agents who were running the show. When she took a good look at *one* of the agents, she gasped. She'd know that tall frame, bee-stung lips, and *short brown hair* anywhere. Ugh! What was *she* doing there?

We've been double-crossed! Theresa thought, her stomach lurching and her lungs ready to burst. She looked over at Caylin and Jo defeatedly, raw terror in her eyes.

"Could it be—," Caylin muttered.

"Surely not," Jo muttered.

"Short Hair!" Theresa screeched, pointing to the woman in horror.

Short Hair glanced over and winked before returning her attention to Jonathon.

"*What?*" Theresa spat out.

"I don't get it," Caylin muttered. "I just don't—"

Suddenly two uniformed men busted in and trained their guns on Short Hair. "Drop your gun or I'll shoot, ma'am," one of them demanded. "Scotland Yard. The jig's up."

Theresa held her breath, terrified of what would happen next.

"Drop the gun, ma'am," Scotland Yard No. 1 repeated, his voice rising with impatience.

"Danielle Hall, Tower," Short Hair said calmly in response.

"Tower?" Jo repeated, shell-shocked.

"Release Mr. Nicholson from your custody, Ms. Hall," Scotland Yard No. 1 demanded.

"But he's guilty!" Jo screeched. "He's a huge part of this whole sick scheme."

"Do what you're told, Ms. Hall," Scotland Yard No. 2 bellowed. "He works for *us*."

"Works for *you*?" Caylin echoed. "But he tried to—"

Scotland Yard No. 1 sighed and showed his identification. "Come on, we're all on the same side here."

Danielle Hall replaced her gun in her holster. To Jo's relief, there were no further surprises.

Scotland Yard No. 1 nodded. "Good work, ladies. You too, son."

Jonathon nodded back, pride shining in his eyes, as two FBI agents set about uncuffing him.

"Wait a minute now, let me get something straight here," Jo began, waving her arms in confusion. "Jonathon Nicholson—the guy who totally tried to grind us into the pavement out there—he's in cahoots with *Scotland Yard?*"

"Scotland Yard," Antonio repeated, sounding just as stunned as Jo felt.

Jonathon walked up to the handcuffed duo and leaned into their faces. "Yes, I work for Scotland

Yard," he said smugly, "and I hope you rot in prison for what you did to my friend Frank Devaroux."

"Well, I'll be darned," Caylin muttered.

"I can't believe it," Theresa whispered.

"Neither can I." Jo shook her head. "*Neither can I.*"

Without a word Caylin embraced Jo and Theresa in a group hug. "We did it," she said, feeling exhausted and exhilarated all at once.

"I never doubted us for a second," Theresa said shakily, then paused. "Well, maybe for a *second.*"

Jo laughed. "Me too," she admitted. "But we made it. For The Tower. For my dad. For *us.*"

Caylin's heart filled with pride. This was better than winning a tournament, a trophy, or even a gold medal. Because tonight they really were world champions.

15

e want all the details, Jonathon," Jo demanded as she cozied up to him at the
World Peace Conference dinner party. If she
didn't get the skinny soon, she was liable to die
of suspense. "How'd you get yourself in this situation?"

"It's kind of long," he said, giving her a shy grin.

"We want every bit of the dirt," Caylin said, her
voice rich with delicious anticipation.

Theresa grinned. "Spare nothing."

"Okay," he said, taking a deep breath. "Frank
Devaroux was this guy I interned with last summer. He was a real genius computer hacker, totally cool, and we kept in touch when I headed
back to school. So a few months ago Dad sent me
some old disks they were about to toss from here
and said I could just erase and use them for
school. But one of the disks had a file on it that
couldn't be erased and actually corrupted my
whole hard drive. I sent everything back here to
Frank, told him what the deal was, and asked
him if he knew what I should do to fix the stuff
it had damaged."

"Was it a virus?" Theresa asked, absolutely fascinated.

Jonathon nodded. "I thought so, but I wasn't sure. So when he got the disk, Frank developed a decoding program to dig into the file. He discovered it was this really elaborate code that took about four or five days to crack, then he finally found that the file contained a list of locations of nuclear warheads in Russia. He knew this list was major."

"I'll say," Theresa agreed as she noticed the gold flecks in Jonathon's eyes. "It's really hard to believe they just had it floating around on an unprotected disk."

"So he destroyed the original, burned the info onto a CD-ROM for the feds, and called a meeting with the heads of the FBI for the next day," he explained. "He hid the disc—I guess in the Green Day case you found—for safety reasons. But later that evening he was killed, anyway. By Alfred and Antonio."

Caylin gasped. "What slimebuckets."

"That'd be a compliment for those guys," Jonathon said solemnly. "We're talking the lowest of the low. So the day Frank died—totally by coincidence—I was here at the embassy to get my computer back from him. That's when Scotland Yard approached me and told me that I, like Frank, was on a list of possible Laqui Bay targets. It wasn't a hit list—just people SY thought they might contact to try to find the disc for them."

"Why you?" Theresa asked.

"Because of my age and my access to the embassy, I guess they figured I'd be an easy target. I wanted time to think about it, but when Frank was murdered that night, I agreed to help. I had no idea that Frank was a special agent for The Tower until after he was killed. Still, I was forbidden to breathe a word of my involvement to anyone—not my father, the CIA, the FBI, *or* The Tower since it was top secret and happening on London soil."

"So why did you do it?" Caylin asked. "I mean, you had to work with the guys who killed your friend."

"It was horrible." Jonathon turned his gaze downward. "I hated pretending I was in league with Laqui Bay. But I wanted to nab those jerks—and I had to get to the list before they did. I did it for Frank . . . and for world peace."

"We were in the same boat," Jo chimed in. "I still can't believe you were on our side all along."

"I know, right?" Jonathon exclaimed, shaking his head in disbelief. "Antonio had me ask the translators if anyone spoke Arabic, thinking that would be bait for anyone who was working for another terrorist group. His theory was that whoever lied about speaking it must have a reason to lie—like wanting to get inside information. So when you bit, Jo, that's when we figured you were a bad guy."

Jo laughed. "I was afraid to lie about that, but I couldn't resist."

"Then right after I discovered the bugs in my suite and office and in Dad's as well," he said. "So we figured you had to have been the one to plant them."

"When it was actually me," Caylin admitted.

"See, I had my suspicions about you but no proof," Jonathon said. "But about Jo we *had* proof—or so we thought. We sent someone to follow Jo, and they saw her with Theresa. So we figured she was working against us, too."

"So then you knew Antonio and Alfred tried to kill us?" Jo asked, finding it hard to believe now that he had anything to do with that. He was so sweet—and *so* cute.

"I didn't know until later," Jonathon said. "I told them up front I'd have no part of anything like that. But when I couldn't find the disc, they threatened to kill my dad. That's when I really started to lose it."

Jo put her hand over his. "I lost my dad. I can understand the pressure."

He smiled gently. "I'm sorry, Jo. No one should have to go through that. And I didn't even lose mine, but I was biting everyone's head off. In fact, I think I yelled at Caylin at least a couple of times. And I didn't even know for sure you were an imposter."

Caylin giggled. "You were *so* mean."

"I know—I'll admit it," he said. "But I was a

basket case. That was a stroke of genius, whoever discovered the Green Day CD location. I was going to give a quick look in there with Antonio because I was desperate, but I'm sure I'd never have found it."

"It was a group brainstorm," Theresa insisted.

"And what a brainstorm it was," Danielle Hall said, breaking away from her conversation with William Nicholson to take a seat with the group.

"And you!" Theresa said with a grin. "I was certain you were trailing us since day one."

"Then you had good instincts," Danielle said, "because I *was* trailing you. Uncle Sam assigned me to be your mentor, so I was never far behind."

Theresa shook her head. "It's such a trip!" she exclaimed. "I just can't believe it."

Danielle smiled. "Well, believe it. I'm your real-life guardian angel—there if you need me or are in a bind. Otherwise laying low and watching from the sidelines."

A waitress approached and delivered a round of virgin strawberry daiquiris, courtesy of William Nicholson.

"I propose a toast," Jonathon said, raising his glass. "To world peace and mistaken identities."

"I'll drink to that!" Jo cheered, clinking glasses with the rest of the gang.

Before Jonathon had a chance to take his first sip, his cell phone rang and he snapped it up.

"Hello? Yes, this is he." He nodded, then grabbed a napkin and furiously scribbled something on it. "Okay, sure, no prob." After he hit the off button, a totally perplexed expression overtook his gorgeous face.

"What's up?" Theresa asked.

"It was a message from someone's uncle Sam," Jonathon announced. "Um, he said you need to turn on channel ninety-six at midnight. And that there's some documentary about Prague he wants you guys to see?"

Jo grinned and grasped her friends' hands in hers. She could feel raw energy, pure excitement, and total empowerment pulsing from one hand to the next. At that moment she would have guessed their hearts were beating in time.

"Are you thinking what I'm thinking?" Theresa asked, a mischievous gleam in her gray eyes.

"Totally," Caylin agreed.

Jo threw her head back and laughed. "Time for another international mission!"

About the Author

Elizabeth Cage is a saucy pseudonym for a noted young adult writer. Her true identity and current whereabouts are classified.

With their maiden mission a smashing success, our three fabulous femmes are slinking on over to Eastern Europe, where a young ballerina has been kidnapped and replaced by a dangerous double. This dancing queen is downright deadly—and she won't stop pirouetting until she kills the prime minister of Varokhastan! Can the Spy Girls stay on their toes long enough to save the peace-loving P.M. from a fatal pas de deux?

**Don't let the action pass you by!
Get your groove on with
Spy Girl mission #2:**

LIVE AND LET SPY

**Coming
mid-October 1998**

Boys. Clothes. Popularity. Whatever!

Based on the major motion picture from Paramount
A novel by H.B. Gilmour
53631-1/$4.99

Cher Negotiates New York 56868-X/$4.99
An American Betty in Paris 56869-8/$4.99
Achieving Personal Perfection 56870-1/$4.99
Cher's Guide to...Whatever 56865-5/$4.99

And Based on the Hit TV Series

Cher Goes Enviro-Mental 00324-0/$3.99
Baldwin From Another Planet 00325-9/$3.99
Too Hottie To Handle 01160-X/$3.99
Cher and Cher Alike 01161-8/$3.99
True Blue Hawaii 01162-6/$3.99
Romantically Correct 01163-4/$3.99
A Totally Cher Affair 01905-8/$4.50
Chronically Crushed 01904-X/$4.99
Babes in Boyland 02089-7/$4.99

Simon & Schuster Mail Order
200 Old Tappan Rd., Old Tappan, N.J. 07675
Please send me the books I have checked above. I am enclosing $_____ (please add
$0.75 to cover the postage and handling for each order. Please add appropriate sales
tax). Send check or money order--no cash or C.O.D.'s please. Allow up to six weeks
for delivery. For purchase over $10.00 you may use VISA: card number, expiration
date and customer signature must be included.

**POCKET
BOOKS**

Name _____

Address _____

City _____ State/Zip _____

VISA Card # _____ Exp.Date _____

Signature _____

1202-10

Think you know everything about today's hottest heartthrob, Leonardo DiCaprio? It's time to take the *ultimate* test of Leo trivia and see if you're truly his number-one fan!

POP

Quiz:
Leonardo DiCaprio

Nancy Krulik

With a special fold-out poster of Leo!

Coming in mid-October 1998

From Archway Paperback
Published by Pocket Books

2019